Library
Brevard Junior College
Cocoa, Florida

THE MARRIAGE OF MADEMOISELLE GIMEL

AND OTHER STORIES

The Marriage of Mademoiselle Gimel
and Other Stories

BY
RENÉ BAZIN

TRANSLATED BY
EDNA K. HOYT

Short Story Index Reprint Series

BOOKS FOR LIBRARIES PRESS
FREEPORT, NEW YORK

First Published 1913
Reprinted 1970

INTERNATIONAL STANDARD BOOK NUMBER:
0-8369-3610-8

LIBRARY OF CONGRESS CATALOG CARD NUMBER:
71-128719

PRINTED IN THE UNITED STATES OF AMERICA

Author's Preface

OF the five stories which compose this collection, the first three have never appeared before. The last two formed, with others, "Donatienne," "Madame Dor," "l'Adjutant," "les Trois Peines d'un Rossignol," a volume published in 1894 under the title of "Humble Amour."

In writing the first version of "Donatienne," that which the *Révue des Deux Mondes* published June 1, 1894, I felt very clearly that I was composing the beginning of a romance. But none of the imagined developments satisfied me. It was not until several years later, about the summer of 1900, that I found in real life, as always, the dénouement of this drama of abandonment. I set myself immediately to work and the story became a romance. The volume of "Humble Amour" was withdrawn from circulation and the copies were destroyed.

That is the strange shipwreck from which I have thought it possible to save two stories which reappear here.

R. B.

Contents

	PAGE
PREFACE	V

THE MARRIAGE OF MADEMOISELLE GIMEL—

I. THE CREAMERY OF MADAME MAULÉON	3
II. THE JOURNAL	23
III. NUMBER 149,007	63
IV. THE DRILL AT BAGATELLE	77
V. THE 12TH OF AUGUST	82
VI. HAUT-CLOS	96
VII. THE DOUBLE VISIT	114

THE DIPLOMAT	123
THE WILL OF OLD CHOGNE	167
THE LITTLE SISTERS OF THE POOR	187
THE RAPHAEL OF MONSIEUR PRUNELIER	249

THE MARRIAGE OF
MADEMOISELLE GIMEL.

THE MARRIAGE OF MADEMOISELLE GIMEL.

I.

THE CREAMERY OF MADAME MAULÉON.

"For a fine day, this is a fine day, Mademoiselle Evelyne! It is like your name! What taste you had to choose such a name."

"Tell that to mamma; you will please her."

"I am not acquainted with her, but I shall not miss the opportunity, if Madame Gimel comes to breakfast here. Evelyne! One sees the person at once, fair, fastidious, distinguished, blue eyes, hair enough to stuff a mattress, and fine and of the true Parisian tint precisely, the nut-brown shade of the year——"

"Madame Mauléon, I am waiting for the bill. I am in a hurry."

"Yes, yes, I understand, I am too familiar. With you there is no making any mistake. Your eyes speak in spite of you; they draw together, they quiver when you are offended, and they dilate to say thank you——"

The tall young girl, standing by the desk, could not keep from laughing.

"It is true," she said, "my companions call me sometimes 'Mademoiselle Folded Eyes'!"

"Oh! what a pretty live doll you are! and prudent, too! Say, Mademoiselle Evelyne, you can spare me two minutes, can't you; I have something—" The mistress of the creamery interrupted herself.

"What are you doing, Louise, place a decanter at No. 4! Monsieur has been waiting for five minutes!"

As she spoke Madame Mauléon bent over to designate the customer at No. 4, and the strapped linen apron, which she wore, parted from her bust and made a pocket. Madame Mauléon loved white. She had white linen sleeves always immaculate, a counter like a professor's desk covered with white porcelain on which, on the left and the right, framing in the mistress and completing the harmony, were piles of plates and bottles of "special cream." On the left also stood Mademoiselle Gimel; her two wrists resting on the counter left both her small gloved hands free, which unconsciously tapped against each other. One could have taken her for a pianist playing an air on an imaginary keyboard; but she was not a musician, simply a typewriter, accustomed to use her fingers, and she was composing this silent phrase:

"You are a gossip, Madame Mauléon! What can you have to say to me? Is it worth while to stay here?"

As she knew, within a few cents, the price of her breakfast, a roll, slice of ham with an egg and

MADEMOISELLE GIMEL 5

a glass of milk, she began spreading the change on the counter.

At this moment a customer came in, whom Madame Mauléon installed with a glance and gave to understand with a nod of the head that he was recognised and was going to be served. She pressed an electric button. Louise, the good-looking little maid, came promptly.

"Wait on No. 1, Louise, and be quick."

Mademoiselle Gimel is a very charming person, in fact, and the customer who has just entered, an under-clerk of the mayor's office in the rue d'Anjou, is already quite persuaded of it. He looks at her with interest while unfolding his paper. Mademoiselle Gimel is simply dressed, but with care, like a Parisian as she is. Her sole luxury is a small bunch of violets pinned to her waist, a white waist, which signifies: "It is the month of July." Her black skirt is like that of so many working-girls, who do not like black, but who are resigned to it, because it is a colour "which does not show dirt." Her straw hat is not worth six francs; but the two roses on the crown were chosen with taste and the mousse-line beneath, the fluff resting on the hair, was charmingly rumpled. Mademoiselle Gimel is twenty-two years old, and she has been at work for ten at least. Her eyes are circled with shadows. Madame Mauléon may think them blue, but she is mistaken; they are flax-grey, with a little of the hue of the flower, if you like, when they open in the full light. One would say that they were intelligent, for they shine; but a clever psychologist or simply a man of the world, who might talk with Mademoiselle Gimel from the Place de la Concorde to the Arc de Triomphe, the Sunday promenade of the stenographer and her mother, would quickly perceive that this pretty girl has less intelligence than decision, that she is proud, that she hides her feelings, and that this little light is the will of a child of Paris, who is not afraid of life, and who looks at it with secret prudence and an amused air. Mademoiselle Gimel is tall and very slender. Her complexion is pale but healthful, her nose slightly turned up and her lips barely pink in repose become smooth and red when she laughs. When she puts her chain of silver-gilt on her neck and goes for her Sunday walk people take her for a fortunate, almost wealthy young woman; the conductor of the omnibus says:

"If you have forgotten your change, Mademoiselle, give your address at the office, that is enough."

She has the discretion of young girls in large cities, which is as real as it is rare, having been shaken and tried. She has a little depth of sadness, like many others, like almost all, but well hidden and well guarded. She has a sensitive nature, forewarned, one who would place her confidence better than her savings, but who has not even been called to make the trial. She is still distrustful with Madame Mauléon herself, she does not make any advances, and that is why she does not seem to attach the least importance to her idle talk. Still, she is no longer as hurried as she appeared to be; she has no embarrassing witness; the mayor's clerk is nothing to her, and the waitress Louise hears nothing when she walks.

"I was going to say to you," resumed Madame Mauléon, "there are many who would like to resemble you. I have an idea that you will not remain Mademoiselle Evelyne very long."

Mademoiselle Gimel stretched out her two hands like a screen to ward off the offer.

"Let us not trifle, Madame Mauléon! In our trade, we have no time to think of the improbable. Here are the ninety centimes."

"And suppose I should tell you that the lieutenant came back here yesterday?"

"Yesterday?"

"Yesterday, he went out almost at the moment when you came in; he was standing on the sidewalk opposite."

Mademoiselle Gimel looked at the mistress of the creamery; and her lashes drooped, and her eyes became soft as if she were looking at a beautiful star; but it was only a moment of oblivion. She smiled.

"I did not see him," she replied; "it is really a pity."

"He saw you very well. He stood there, outside, opposite the door, as if there had been an accident in the street, all the time I suppose that you were standing still visible above the curtains."

"And then?"

"He went away."

"Well, so much the better! *Au revoir*, Madame Mauléon."

"Till to-morrow, Mademoiselle Evelyne."

The young girl went out, followed the rue Boissy d'Anglas, on which the creamery was situated, and went up the Boulevard Malesherbes. She walked very slowly. It was ten minutes after one, and, provided that she was at Maclarey's bank by twenty-five minutes past, she would still be five minutes ahead of Mademoiselle Raymonde and of Mademoiselle Marthe, who breakfasted at their home in the Ternes quarter.

The intense heat of the sun softened the asphalt. Joy dwelt in this summer light, made for the growth of life, and it made more rapid and more elastic the gait of the promenaders of every age who were going up or going down the boulevard. Carriages fanned the driveway and sent the white dust up to the third stories. Rising above the noise of horns, sirens, and wheels, the wrangling of two men caused Evelyne to stop. An auto had come near upsetting a cab. The coachman abused the chauffeur; professional rivalry made sharp words. The driver cried: "Beast of an aristocrat! Get out, old caravan! Get out, smoke all the time!"

The chauffeur mocked: "Look at his muddy wheels! To the stable, old man, to the stable!"

The passers-by laughed, grouped themselves around the place where the auto, a wonderful mahogany-coloured machine, finishing its curve with the gliding motion of a ship coming into port, drew up and stopped an inch from the side-

MADEMOISELLE GIMEL 9

walk. Evelyne had never seen so spacious a coach before! The chauffeur's seat, a coupé and behind the coupé, separated by a glass, a third compartment.

"That is for the companion," explained a workman. Evelyne was in the front row, admiring the interior arrangement, the bevelled glasses, the deep-yellow silk upholstery, the pocket stuffed with maps, the spy-glass lodged in a leather case on the ceiling, and then, on the roof, the trunks and the complete set of tires, stowed away like coils of rope upon a ship's bridge.

"How far that must be able to go!" said she. "One would like to be the companion."

"Well! Mademoiselle, if I were the owner, your place would be in the inside, for sure."

She had spoken aloud then? She turned her head, put on her offended air, her eyebrows drawn together, and saw a young clerk with a fine beard and a shrewd profile, a bookbinder, engraver, decorator, something of a jester in any case, and an artist, standing in the rear, a portfolio under his arm; then, bursting into a laugh:

"Thanks," she said; "I would rather not ride!"

She made her way through the group, which opened before this pretty, smiling girl. She did not appear to notice the slight bow of the fine bearded head and went on her way quickly in the sunlight.

She would have liked to go in the Parc Monceau and make the tour of a grass-plot; it was her chosen walk; she took out her watch and turned short to the left; it was impossible to take such a liberty. The management of the bank had sent an urgent piece of work to the typewriter's office. If Evelyne were late, Mademoiselle Raymonde, as an elder clerk, would not fail to remark to Monsieur Maclarey that Mademoiselle Evelyne took most extraordinary liberties, "no doubt because she was pretty." Ah! what unpardonable inequality! Nearly all the difficulties of her position came to Mademoiselle Gimel because of her charming face, and of that something besides, which makes a woman, even one of equal beauty, jealous of another.

While she was walking toward the Maclarey bank, customers filled the creamery: a few workmen—as they could only be served with water, milk, and beer, they were rare at Madame Mauléon's—post-office clerks, a bookkeeper of a wholesale confectionery shop, a young man, either a student or young lawyer, unless he were an underwriter, for he always carried a morocco bag under his arm, which, on entering, he placed on a chair with his gloves and silk hat—eleven customers in all. The small hall was nearly full. There remained but one vacant place. Madame Mauléon, magnificent with satisfaction, brightened up at the clicking of plates, lowering her head and presenting her bands of brown hair to the reflections of the light, her eyes half closed over the easy accounts, or else she held out a saucer, a cup, a plate, reassured with a gesture a hurried customer, or reproved in an undertone Louise, the only waitress. The latter did wonders. She had a way of gliding over the flagstones, sprinkled with sawdust, of pushing open the kitchen door

MADEMOISELLE GIMEL

with her foot, coming back with four or five orders, distributing them without ever making a mistake; she had an elastic step, a sure movement, black eyes which saw everything, a quick way of saying: "I know, I will be back in a moment," which would have excited the admiration of a head waiter. You must realise that there were no experts in this hall. No one dreamed of paying the compliments, which she so well deserved, to the little maid. She heard other praises, discreet on account of the presence of Madame Mauléon; she listened to them with indifference, as one who lacks time. She was no fool. When the post-office clerk, having sweetened his coffee, drew from his pocket and arranged in fan shape five lottery tickets for the benefit of the "Scrofulous children of the Seine," and asked, "Mademoiselle Louise, if you please, choose two tickets for me, so that I will win; the others I give back," she replied:

"Choose for yourself!"

"No, you have a lucky hand. If I win——"

"You will divide?"

"Well, not exactly, but I will give you a kiss."

"Don't trouble! You would get two big prizes at once."

She took away the coffee-pot and every one laughed. Madame Mauléon herself approved, because the jesting had not interfered with the service. The clerk went out, the fan of tickets still open in his fingers. At the same moment, the lieutenant entered. He was in citizen's dress. Without responding to the inclination of

Madame Mauléon's head, without even appearing to notice it, he seated himself before a table upon which the hors-d'œuvres were served, and began crunching a piece of an artichoke. You saw, under his moustache, his teeth, which were white, pointed, and glistening. You would have said that he was smiling. He ate like all young and ravenous beings, who always have the air of attacking a prey. He was one of those men, numerous in France, whom one can call born soldiers. His brown eyes, under the clearly and strongly framed forehead, beneath the straight, short, abruptly ending eyebrows, seemed void of curiosity. When you caught their gaze you felt that you were in the presence of a disciplined soul, a logical and strong mind, which ideas interested little and never disturbed. A street urchin called after him one day:

"There goes a defender!"

He had guessed rightly; he was a man of humble origin, but he carried in his breast the image of France and the little lamp lighted before it. His features were regular, but rudely moulded; the jaw, for instance, a trifle advancing and square-cut in front, lifted at a right angle near the ear, the bone showing everywhere near the skin. His thin, short moustache, which he tried to twist and curl at the corners of his lips, proclaimed youth and youthful pride. He must have been the son of some subordinate official, or of a retired non-commissioned officer or small landed proprietor, one of those who have learned early in life that they must have a career and live by it, and who at once have chosen the army, knowing that it would leave them poor, but preferring it to all others because it satisfied in them a passion for authority, honour, and action. They bring with them to the regiment the love of order, of minute preparation for the smallest enterprises, of manual tasks, strict economy, and also a facility for fellowship with soldiers, a willingness to do a service, valuable in barrack or camp life. Like the real nobility, though for other reasons, they have been—they are—the strength, the traditional element of command, the normal staff of the army. Often they go through the schools. Often they enlist. They are methodical, serious, and brave. A chief who knows the species, and who does not clash with them, can make heroes of them. They talk little; when they have the leisure, they dream, but sentiment is a subordinate thing.

Louis Morand had not been for very long a customer of Madame Mauléon. She knew but little about him, not to say that she knew nothing. Such a condition of things could not continue: the habits of the mistress would not permit it. When the lieutenant had finished his breakfast, he approached the counter and Madame Mauléon smiled.

"Monsieur le Lieutenant was late to-day, and I imagine he was hungry."

Louis Morand made a slight inclination.

"It belongs to your age," resumed the mistress of the creamery, seeing that she received no other response than the pieces of coin rapidly laid on the counter.

The majority of the customers had left the shop. Madame Mauléon insisted:

"And then, your profession, too. You drill some distance from here, I wager."

"At Bagatelle or at Issy-les-Molineaux," said Monsieur Morand finally.

"As far as that? And ninety in the shade! You have run about! I am not surprised that you have a good appetite."

She was delighted to have obtained a word from the lieutenant. She smiled, she exulted, she wished to detain this uncommunicative customer, and, recalling him with a sweeping wave of the hand, for he had turned to go:

"Well, Monsieur le Lieutenant, I assure you that I have some customers who do not often breathe 'the fresh air' of the country. For instance, the pretty stenographer of Maclarey's bank——"

He knit his brows and said carelessly, but without seeking to leave the desk:

"I do not know whom you mean."

"Why, yes; the young girl who came in the other day, as you were going out. She breakfasts always before you do; you looked at her, from the sidewalk yonder. A young girl such as one does not often see, I assure you; she is pretty, she is discreet, she is a workwoman."

The lieutenant's lips lengthened a fraction of an inch abruptly and immediately regained the normal line.

"Well, au revoir, Madame Mauléon!"

"Au revoir, Monsieur le Lieutenant. Till another time."

He did not even hear. He gained the door, with a serious air, with his marching step, preoccupied with giving a favourable idea of the French army, of its dignity, of the good use it makes of its time, to the three remaining customers, who were watching the officer go out.

"It did not hinder him," thought Madame Mauléon, "from casting a glance at the table which I pointed out to him, and which is the one where Mademoiselle Evelyne sits. He remembered, then, something. He is a very worthy young man, but cold. My Mauléon would not have gone away so quickly, if one had spoken to him of a young girl. He had the artistic temperament! This one—I do not know——"

She weighed these thoughts, her eyes lifted toward the windows, which poured into the creamery the almost dazzling light of the rue Boissy d'Anglas.

It was the hour when Paris trembles less, vibrates less, when its noise diminishes, when, in the four thousand veins which are its streets, the current of life slackens and the fever falls. It was oppressively warm. People passing walked upon the heated asphalt and felt their heels sinking into the sidewalk. Many employees dozed while watching the shop, office, or factory. It was the hour for resuming work in yards and bureaus. There were young heads which, in crossing the threshold, turned for an instant toward the blue line of the sky from which life flowed.

Mademoiselle Gimel entered the room where the three typewriters of the bank worked when the dictation of correspondence or the session of a board of management did not call them into one of the offices. Three tables ranged along the wall near the windows, three chairs, three machines, a box and row of pegs in the rear, furnished the room. Evelyne took off her hat.

"Are you hot, my dear? Has any one followed you?"

The young girl tossed back her hair, and, without replying, seated herself before the second machine.

The same voice continued:

"You know it is not becoming to you! You are as red——!"

The occupant of the table nearest the door, Mademoiselle Raymonde, had ceased to write on seeing Evelyne enter, and, leaning back, looked at her with an expression which she thought to make mocking, but which, in spite of her, betrayed her soul full of suffering and revolt. This little woman, nearing forty, all nerves and eyes, felt that she was vanquished, or on the point of being so, and she avenged herself on life by detesting some one. Mademoiselle Raymonde was the oldest stenographer of the firm, something like the chief of stenography. She was vain of this; she could say to Evelyne or to Marthe, her two companions in the office: "I am established, Mesdemoiselles, I am the head here," but she did not know that Monsieur Maclarey cared little for length of service; that what he exacted was swiftness of touch, exactitude, the power of divining, the delicacy of ear for distinguishing words indistinctly uttered or stammered when he dictated, and which all these virtuosi lose gradually; an old cashier, yes, but an old stenographer, no. She felt a grudge against Mademoiselle Marthe and Mademoiselle Evelyne for being young, and against Mademoiselle Evelyne, in addition, for being pretty. She had noticed, from the first day, the preferences of the employees of the bank for this tall clerk who walked like a lady on the carpet of the council room, and who carried her young head proudly.

Mademoiselle Raymonde had that flabby and half-faded look which one remarks so often in women of the world who keep too late hours, hair weary of being blondined and undulated, a complexion that required powder, pale lips and eyelids. But, at this moment, this little image of crackled Dresden china, reanimated by anger, was also rejuvenated by it. In spite of the heat, Mademoiselle Raymonde had on her shoulders a boa of silk gauze which was becoming to her; with her exasperated and trembling right hand she was pinching the end of the boa.

"Presently," said she, "when they send to ask for a stenographer for the Board of Oilworks of Mogador, do me the favour not to offer your services. That is my right."

"Why, I do not dispute it!" Evelyne answered. "I never offer my services. As if the Oilworks of Mogador were so amusing!"

"Enough, we know you!"

Mademoiselle Marthe, very dark, her hair parted in the middle, and whom one might have taken for a student, came into the room to resume her work. As she was very stiff in her movements, her companions had nicknamed her Monolyth.

"Isn't it true, Monolyth, we know this young lady? She has ways of attracting the attention, of gaining the favour of the officials. We know by what means you succeed!"

Evelyne, whom the walk had put in a good humour, shrugged her shoulders.

"Then imitate me!"

Mademoiselle Marthe had a smile of contempt, which drew downward her soft lips and eyelids with their long lashes. The undulation and the crackling noise of the moving sheets of paper was heard, then the dry click of a letter striking the sheet, then ten, then a hundred minute blows, all alike, answering to each other. The three women had begun to typewrite. The door opened. Young Monsieur Amédée, one of the exchange clerks, thrust through the half-opening his square head, which he tried to lengthen by a too thin, pointed beard, and which revealed the whole framework of his jaw and throat.

"Mesdemoiselles, one of you, if you please, for the Board of Oilworks——"

"Here, Monsieur, I will go!"

But the young man, as if he had not heard Mademoiselle Raymonde, continued:

"Mademoiselle Evelyne, will you come?"

Evelyne arose. She avoided looking at her companions and carried with her her stenographic book. The little keyboards behind her began to click furiously. Then one of the typewriters stopped and burst into tears.

The afternoon came to an end; the light faded very slowly away; the heat continued stifling. When night had come, the windows, one by one, opened upon that impalpable furnace of dust, which men, animals, machines and vibrations of pavements and of walls send up through the cuts of the streets. Each of the cells, rich or poor, where men live, one above the other, was connected thus, more closely, with this great troubled current of movement and of noise which bathes our houses until the hours of approaching day. Each received, at the same time, a little of the fresh air which fell in waves into the furnace. That did not waken thought, but it took away the terror which the solitude of night has for many; it sufficed to preserve the semi-sleep of dream and repose.

Madame Gimel, who lived on the fourth floor, rue Saint-Honoré, not far from the Nouveau Cirque, like everybody else, had opened the window of her room. She was sitting near the balcony; she saw well enough, thanks to gas-jets and reflections from façades, to run the tucks in a white waist, which she was finishing. She worked until five o'clock in the office of a wholesale house in the vicinity of the bank, and, in the evening, she found time to do some fine lingerie sewing. In the background, in the shadow, some one was silent and was thinking. Madame Gimel, now and then, straightened up; she turned her head, and, although she only saw the outlines of a motionless form reclining in the easy chair, she brightened up. She asked:

"Don't you want to light the lamp?"

"What is the use, Mamma? The twilight rests me so much. I think that it is delicious."

"I don't."

A half moment passed. In the abyss of the street below the huge omnibus of Ternes shrieked out, its four wheels suddenly blocked; wordless oaths, snortings of motor, murmurs of cockneys rose in waves. Then, as if the wave had broken, there was a lull, a dull rumbling, and a little tremor of the earth shaken by the retreat of the heavy masses, which were again set in motion.

"I do not complain—I was thinking of the time when you will be married!"

"I do not look so far as you. Would you be pleased?"

"Not too much so! I have only you, but for all that you are old enough."

"Twenty-two years, yes, past, and what have I besides?"

"Everything: a Parisian's courage, a trade, good looks, white teeth—yes, indeed, whoever wants pearls, a real necklace, two rows, not one false!"

"But, Mamma, it is only the men who do not marry who admire them! What ideas you have this evening, indeed!"

In the depths of the room, Evelyne laughed, and her white teeth threw a little light in the shadow. There were the white margins of an engraving and an ivory statue, a finger high, which shone in the same way. Evelyne, seated in a low chair, had placed on her dress and abandoned to the folds of the stuff her hands, which shone also, very vaguely. She asked, and Madame Gimel guessed that her daughter was no longer laughing:

"Then, your presentiment of marriage is based upon nothing?"

"Upon nothing at all."

"Curious, isn't it? I have one quite similar to offer to you. No reason for it, and my heart not in it. It must be the effect of the heat."

She rose and went to the older woman, who dropped her work and raised her arms. Near the window, without caring about the neighbours, in the twilight which the street sent up, Evelyne kissed Madame Gimel, who kept the fair head near her white head, thinking of all the happiness of the past, as if an event had marked its end; while Evelyne was thinking of all the happiness to come, although she loved no one and nothing was changed in her life. And they did not talk with each other any more when they separated, when Evelyne had seated herself, turning her back to the street, by the side of her mother, and the latter had picked up her needle again, whose little regular clicking was lost, like so many other sounds, in the noise of the city. They were thinking, both of them, about the marriage of Evelyne. And, all vague as it was, this thought divided them already. Madame Gimel was thinking that if Evelyne should marry the shoemaker, Quart-de-Place, or some one else, the intimacy of twenty years would not continue, in spite of the vow that Evelyne, in her moments of expansion, made with so grave, so ardent a voice, with her whole soul in her eyes:

"If he wishes to separate me from you, I refuse him!"

Evelyne, who had less imagination, was simply reviewing in her mind the words of the mistress of the creamery; she did not attach any importance to them; still, she would have liked to know if they would come to anything.

"More astonishing things have happened," she thought. "If I were loved, it seems to me that I would recognise quickly if he only thinks me a pretty woman, or indeed—and I would love him only on this condition—if he has confidence in me, if he understands that I can be a friend, a power, a helpmeet, a true woman, and even a lady, why not?"

Time slipped away; she gave no thought at all to Madame Gimel. And for this reason, two or three times, she reproached herself for the egotism of this idleness and this silence, putting her hand upon the hands of her mother, who stopped her sewing, much touched.

In the room, whose ceiling was low and which was of average width, Madame Gimel had contrived to place all the furniture which she had inherited from her husband: a sofa and four chairs of green velvet, an ebony sideboard, which she believed to be of the Renaissance, a standing bed of the same style, which was covered by a counterpane also of green velvet intersected by two bands of hand embroidery. The room was gloomy; but Madame Gimel thought it the height of good taste. When the daylight waned, the cardboard margins, which framed the photograph hanging opposite the bed, took on an extraordinary importance, and made a sort of halo around the portrait of the late Monsieur Gimel, late adjutant in the Republican Guard.

II.

THE JOURNAL.

Like so many others of her condition in life, Evelyne Gimel kept a journal in which she jotted down, although irregularly, certain little events of her life, dates, poems she had read, and "impressions of plays." The journal had thirty-two pages in all. It was suddenly increased by ten new pages. And this is what they recorded:

"Saturday, July 6, 190—.
"This morning, something new happened to me. I do not dare say pleasant, for one never knows, when one has no dot and is a little pretty, whether to be pleased with an attention or to be offended. But, in spite of myself, I do not feel offended. In the first place, he appeared very serious; he does not joke with Madame Mauléon; I have observed him; he does not even pay any attention to the people who enter, who leave, or to little Louise, who waits. That is precisely

what began to interest me; he looked only at me. I arrived late at the creamery. I had taken quite a walk in the Parc Monceau, on leaving Maclarey's, at the risk of being scolded by the amiable Raymonde. The reason? Merely the memory of that jest of Madame Mauléon, who insisted that this officer, her customer, had noticed me for a moment when he left the shop. In meeting him, I would see. Well, he was there at his table; he looked at me at the moment when I entered. I came late for him, but he did not know that. Nor can I say that he showed any emotion, or admiration; but, when he saw that I too looked at him—oh! just as at the others—he lowered his eyes; he did not 'insist,' and that is already very nice; it is a proof that he does not think lightly of me. I took my seat at the table in front of the desk, near the mirror. Madame Mauléon devoured me with glances under her eyelids, she assassinated me with smiles. She had the air of saying to me:

"'At last, little one, you have come at the hour when he breakfasts, bravo! But turn your head then, just a trifle, to the right.'

"I did not appear to understand her. However, in the mirror on the left, without needing to make the slightest movement, I saw the whole room. I had no difficulty in discovering that I was the object of a study. He proceeded stealthily, with little glances, when he supposed that I could not see him. I am well aware that the creamery does not offer many subjects of interest. Three, at the most: myself, a clerk from Piver's, who is not ugly, and a maker of fancy trimmings, whom I have already met and who is not very shy. He only looked at me, but discreetly, as if I intimidated him. I, to intimidate any one! It seems to me that that is curious. A compliment would have flattered me less. I was the first to leave. I do not think that I took ten minutes to eat my breakfast."

"Monday, July 8.
"I have seen him again. This time, he scarcely lifted his eyes in my direction; but he did not look anywhere else. Madame Mauléon called me to her, when she saw that I meant to pay little Louise for my breakfast.

"'I believe, in truth, that he is interested in you, Mademoiselle Evelyne. Yesterday, Sunday, you were not here, naturally—he asked me for all sorts of information.'

"'What about? About whom?'

"'About you! What you did? Have I known you for a long time? How old you were precisely?'

"'That is droll.'

"I said, 'That is droll'; I thought very differently. But I laughed in order not to appear too naïve.

"'Twenty-two years, my dear Madame Mauléon, and virtue enough to distrust men who think me good looking.'

"My heart was troubled, in truth. It takes so little, even when one believes that they are sure of themselves."

"Tuesday, July 9.

"I took a long time to breakfast on an egg and a piece of bread! No one came, since he did not come. Am I forgotten already?"

"Monday, July 15, ——.

"The day after our national festival. For me the festival is to-day. For eight days I had no news. And, this morning, oh! I not only have seen him again, he has spoken to me; he has almost confessed to me. And even wholly, I believe. I write to be more sure, to be able to reflect better on the meaning of the words, on the details, in reading over my journal; perhaps also for the pleasure that there is, when a feeling is born in your heart, to confide it to something, for lack of some one. Very well, I was the first to enter and I had not been there more than five minutes when he himself came in. At the first glance, I comprehended not only that he sought me, but that this meeting was going to be a date in my life. We were almost alone; only a chance customer with us, and then the little perfumery clerk from Piver's, who was looking at her beefsteak with her near-sighted eyes. Madame Mauléon turned pale, as happens when she makes a mistake in a bill. Monsieur Morand seated himself on the left, as I was on the right of the room, and plunged into the reading of a paper. But I plainly saw that he was not reading; he never moved his eyes from the title of an article; he did not give any order to the maid standing near him, and who, unoccupied for a moment, moved in

MADEMOISELLE GIMEL

measure her rosy head, her left foot and the folded napkin, which she carried upon the radius (I learned that word at school), as if to say:

"'When will Monsieur le Lieutenant deign to see that I am here!'

"He did not see anything. The little clerk from Piver's having gone, Madame Mauléon, who is not stupid, moved in her white box and said:

"'Monsieur le Lieutenant, you promised to bring me a souvenir of your country!'

"He trembled like a man who hears his condemnation—I imagine—and stammered, embarrassed, trying to smile and searching in his pocket:

"'To be sure, Madame, I think I have some here with me——'

"He rose, while little Louise stepped aside to let him pass, and went toward the desk of Madame Mauléon, my friend, and I saw that he showed her a series of sketches, or postal cards, and she thanked, and he explained, and I heard words cut with exclamations, a sort of duo, almost as incomprehensible as the words of a chorus at the opera:

"'Perfectly, my mother is alone.'

"'Fifty years?'

"'No, fifty-seven.'

"'What a pretty little country!'

"'What are you saying! Large, immense, Madame Mauléon! And here is— We were two— Scarcely enough to live.—Content all the same! Come now! It is called the Valromey.'

"'What did you say?'

"'Valromey, an old word; the valley of the Romans.'

"A ray of sunshine touched the mirror on the left and rebounded from the counter onto the shoulder of the mistress of the creamery. Madame Mauléon leaned forward.

"'Mademoiselle Evelyne, come and look at these pretty post-cards that Monsieur Morand has brought me. Monsieur Louis Morand, Lieutenant of the 28th, of the line.'

"He turned around, bowed very low, as people of good society do when they are presented to a lady, and, with a decision, an audacity, that I had not the time to enjoy, and which confused me at once, he gathered up the postal cards and came to me:

"'If they would interest you, Mademoiselle, I should be most happy.'

"What a situation! I was breakfasting, or I was making a pretence, I had a knife, a fork, a glass before me and I have no idea what, on my plate, and it is at this moment, without my being able to foresee anything, that Monsieur Louis Morand spoke to me for the first time! I had so little suspected that this moment was near or even possible, that I had put on my every-day waist, and even, under my straight collar, a bright blue tie, that mamma gave me, and which I do not like. I rose, I took three steps, not to approach nearer to him, but to place myself behind the neighbouring table, which was unoccupied and clean, and I said:

"'Certainly, Monsieur, I should be pleased to look at them. We will be better here——'

"I felt myself stupid and timid, which is not usual with me. I am certain that I must have had the air of a boarding-school miss, as they say; I, who have never been to any but the primary —and there as day pupil! I looked down. He followed me and seated himself, not in front of me, but by my side, very near. He is taller than I by a head. He spread out ten postal cards on the marble table, like a game. He had the air of guessing that he held the trump.

"'A country no doubt unknown to you, Mademoiselle, the Ain: some mountains, as you see: the Dent du Chat, the Colombier; on this side, Lake Bourget—do you like it, Mademoiselle?'

"'I know so little of the country, Monsieur. I know nothing but the rue Saint-Honoré, fancy!'

"I dared not look at him. The hand which he had placed upon the table contracted, then stretched out again and took a new picture. He has a long, thin hand, small joints and the articulations strongly knit; it is the hand of a strong and of a sentimental man. Madame Mauléon, motionless with anxiety, must have questioned my face.

"'Then, look at this, Mademoiselle. It is the high valley of Valromey; if you should go there, you would be astonished at least, I am sure. There are little villages huddled in a fresh and green cave which the wind of the mountains fills. In winter, we often have three feet of snow.'

"He hesitated a moment, took up a fresh postal card, turned it over, and, placing his finger on a light greyish spot:

"'That is our house. It is as well known there as the Louvre is in Paris. My mother lives there still, alone, now that I am gone. Madame Théodore Morand.'

"Why did he tell me that? The tone of his voice had suddenly become different. I raised my head, not much, just enough for my glance, from the corner of my eyes, to meet the eyes of Monsieur Morand. This lieutenant is a singular man; he was as pale, his expression as severe, as if he had challenged me to a duel. He waited for my reply as if his phrase had had a significance of great importance. And I believe, in truth, that what he wished to say was:

"'It is there that the one who will be my wife will live some day, and if you would listen well, Mademoiselle, to my heart, which is so near yours, you would hear your name.'

"I did hear it, Monsieur, but I belong to Paris, and I am a clerk, earning her living; that is two reasons to be distrustful. I pretended not to understand, thinking that he would repeat his thought more clearly if I did so. And I said:

"'Indeed, no, the farthest I have been is to Bagnolet.'

"He looked at me with more attention, to see if I were intelligent, and very likely also he found that I did not express myself in very pure French. For his face wore a smile, swift as the turn of the wheel of an auto. Then, carelessly, he gathered up the post-cards, even those that I had not seen:

"'I beg your pardon, Mademoiselle, for having shown you things so uninteresting to you.'

"'But how so, Monsieur? I meant no offence: quite the contrary.'

"He returned to his place and I went back to mine. Madame Mauléon, very agitated, and who always thinks that she does not show it, began to contemplate the sun through the windows. I did not swallow a mouthful more, I left a portion of cherries in the saucer. The lieutenant drank his cup of coffee at a single draught and he went out, without saying a word to the mistress of the creamery. Passing by me, he made a military salute, just as he would have saluted Madame Mauléon, nothing more, nothing less.

"As soon as he had closed the door, I rose in my turn. All this had not taken long.

"'Explain yourself, Madame Mauléon, what does this mean?'

"'That he loves you, my child.'

"'Speak lower, you have a customer.'

"'He is deaf. But how pale you are! What is the matter?'

"'It is cold here.'

"'Seventy degrees; you call that cold? Come, confess now. You like him, too.'

"'You are joking; I do not even know him!'

"'One loves always before knowing. And besides, you are going to know him; he wishes for nothing but that. Come nearer, that Louise may not hear; he asks you for a rendezvous.'

"'Me! But I am not one of that kind!'

"'You are angry? You do not know him, indeed! Very well! Here are the exact words which he said to me, I repeat them to you: "You will ask, Madame Mauléon, if Mademoiselle Gimel will do me the honour to grant me ten minutes' conversation."'

"'He said: "the honour?"'

"'Why, yes.'

"'You are very sure?'

"'I hear him still; the honour, the honour, I would take an oath to it!'

"'Then, I must accept. The honour! The motive is good then! It is. Ah! I beg you, Madame, do not give me false joy. I am only a poor girl. I seem to joke often, but it is because I must. I am sensitive, to the bottom of my heart.'

"'Like me!'

"'To be loved for one's self, that is a thing that one always wishes for. When it comes like that, suddenly, you understand.'

"'Yes, you are crying.'

"'No, I am laughing, you see I am.'

"'It comes to the same thing, little one! Whether one laughs, whether one cries, the heart knows no longer what it is doing. What must I answer him, your—sweetheart?'

"'Not yet! I do not know whether I shall please him, after he has talked with me. Where do you advise me to meet him? Ah! mamma will be happy! Not at home, just the same!'

"'No, he wishes to speak, at first, with you alone, neither here at my place, nor at your home; some quiet place, away from taxicabs.'

"'The Place de la Concorde, then, by the side of the statue. Oh! no, that is impossible; all my young friends cross there.'

"'Go a hundred steps farther; he will wait for you near the greenhouse of the Tuileries, on the terrace at the right, on the side of the Seine, at half-past six?'

"'Yes, that will do!'

"'The place is perfect. Up to eight o'clock, one still finds children with their nurses there. They will not be astonished, you know. They are used to it. And on what day?'

"'Why, to-morrow! why put it off? Does he not wish the meeting for to-morrow?'

"The mistress of the creamery began to laugh:

"'What put that idea in your head? Why, no! He is more in love than you are, more in a hurry to tell you than you are to hear him; and when I shall tell him "to-morrow," he will say: "Why not to-day?"'

"I felt that great joy which pierces through and which betrays itself, whatever one may do. Often I had said to myself:

"'I may perhaps love, but I will not show it; that is too silly!'

"I feel that I have not kept my word. 'To be loved,' I tasted these words as, formerly, I would let a sugar-plum dissolve in my mouth. Did the passing people look at me more than usual? Those who carry a joyous secret imagine that they are transparent. Perhaps they are not wrong. At the bank, I could not keep still. That silly Marthe, who thinks herself artistic because she wears her hair parted *à la Vierge*, did not fail to remark that I went four times to ask explanations of Monsieur Amédée, whose report

I was copying; but Raymonde, who is more clever and more malicious, took the finished report from the table, under pretext of examining it, and carried it herself to the young secretary. I let her do it. She remained a long time—she came back with her eyes more red than usual. It seems that she made the most incredible scene. I have the details from Monsieur Amédée himself, he told me at the door—a scene of jealousy! It is too absurd!

"'There is really, Monsieur, a preference given to Mademoiselle Evelyne which I cannot explain. I am the senior clerk and the reports are confided to her. There is no use in being devoted! I do not know whether you have remarked, Monsieur, that this silly girl becomes more and more giddy? To-day her thoughtlessness exceeds all bounds.'

"Here she became much affected.

"'I have, however, demanded information from a friend of mine, in the loan establishment, where Monsieur Amédée worked before coming to Maclarey's. You will pardon me for being so frank. I asked her if you were capable of—how shall I express it?—of favouring one stenographer because she is younger and more coquettish? She answered me:

"'"I do not think so, he is a settled man." And yet, Monsieur, whenever there is any important work, it is Mademoiselle Evelyne who has it!'

"She began weeping. Monsieur Amédée declared that he would rather direct thirty men than three women, and he left Mademoiselle Raymonde to dry her tears.

"All that because I seemed happy. I was happy in fact, and I am so still. At the late hour in which I am writing this, my mother is asleep in her room next to mine. I feel that sleep will not visit me so soon. She has guessed something too, dear mamma! While we were dining to-day together, in the kitchen, she noticed, at first, that I ate with the appetite of a young wolf, or of an errand-girl, and that, nevertheless, I forgot to eat, at intervals, to look out of the window!

"'Whom are you laughing at, Evelyne?'

"'No one.'

"'Yes, you are.'

"'See for yourself; the windows on the opposite court are all closed, in spite of the heat.'

"'Then you are laughing at your thoughts? I know how that is!'

"She was silent, and I understood that she was treading many silent paths, that she was searching in all of the houses in which I might have, according to her, a suitor. Poor mamma! As if Paris was the same for her and for me! She did not wish to say so, but she suffered also at the thought that I was not confiding in her. For myself, I did not wish, I do not wish to say anything, because I am not certain. Such a love! Is it possible? I, the insignificant stenographer? How I wish it were to-morrow evening! Ah! to-morrow evening, if he has spoken to me as I dare not believe that he will speak, then, I will be expansive. Yes, I will share my joy with her, I will atone for the pain I have given her to-day. Mamma said to me:

"'The shoemaker's son, our neighbour, when I came in this evening gave me a friendly nod; it is not the first time; I am sure that he thinks of you.'

"'Quart-de-Place?'

"'Why do you call him that? Poor boy!'

"'It is the name he gives to all those who do not deal with his father.'

"'Yes, more than once I have seen him, on turning a little, when I passed, I have seen him devouring you with his eyes.'

"'That leaves me untouched, Mamma.'

"'Without doubt, but does it leave you indifferent?'

"'Oh! you talk like! . . . No, I beg your pardon, I mean absolutely untouched.'

"Poor dear mamma did not reply; but she had that little contraction of the mouth which is the sign with her of a blow received, the 'touch' of the fencing-master. It gave me pain to be the cause of it. But what could I do? We separated earlier than usual. She cannot be asleep, either. She is thinking: 'Children are ungrateful, yes, all of them!'

"No, it is not true. I am grateful to her, on the contrary, because she has been a true mother, a mother for whom her child is not a plaything to be dressed and kissed, but a love which changes the whole life. I was 'big as your hand'—how often I have heard her say that! I was 'delicate,' I was 'lively as a mouse with blue eyes.' Mamma was afraid, if she gave me to a nurse in the country, that I would not be well taken care of. She was no longer young when she married the 'handsome Gimel,' my father, whom I have scarcely known. A little tremor of fear and the great sacrifice was at once accomplished. Mamma, who had a good place, mamma, who was a saleswoman at Revillon's, gave up her place for Evelyne. She has never been separated from me, and all that she has gained, alas, is that I do not even tell her, this evening, that it is joy that keeps me awake. Poor mamma! Her husband, retired adjutant of the Republican Guard, was never, I imagine, a vigorous worker. He had his pension. He used to say: 'I am looking for employment in civil life.'

"Mamma said nothing; but she embroidered, she took in sewing, she earned what was lacking for the home and the right to keep the 'little one' with her. Thanks to her, we have never suffered for anything. She even claims that we will end by being 'quite at our ease.'

"I laugh at that this evening. We have not become rich. And here I am loved! Is it not mysterious? Could I ever have dreamed that an officer would fall in love with me, just for having seen me at Madame Mauléon's eating little pink radishes! He must have guessed that I had been well brought up, by a courageous, clearheaded woman, loving her Paris, which does not spoil her but which amuses her, and that I was a modest girl, born of an admirable mother. Ah! if we should marry, he and I, he would have to be polite and attentive to mamma. No superciliousness! No false pride! I shall tell him that to-morrow with other things, many others."

"Half past twelve, ——.

"I have no desire to sleep. I must go to bed, however, because the stenographer must be at work to-morrow morning at nine o'clock. We are given no leave on account of love. I can see Monsieur Maclarey's face, if I should say to him:

"'I have a sweetheart; will you permit me to leave an hour before the others?'

"He would ask himself if I had taken leave of my common sense. And Monsieur Amédée? He would insert his monocle to make sure that I am indeed Mademoiselle Gimel, stenographer, esteemed for her regular application and her good humour, and he would answer with his diplomatic air:

"'Do not forget, Mademoiselle, that the copy of the report on the Loan of Herzegovina has been intrusted to you because you are the least frivolous of our stenographers.'

"But, just the same, at six o'clock, I fly and without waiting for Mademoiselle Raymonde!"

"Tuesday, July 16.

"Since noon, I have not lived. I have always been proud of my self-control, but I am so no longer. I have always believed that I would not let myself be carried away, and my heart beat madly, foolishly, as soon as I thought: 'half past six, the Tuileries, Louis Morand'; and I thought of nothing else, and I had to exert all my will and a tiresome attention, not to mix these words in the copy of the coal-mine and financial reports which I was copying for the bank!

MADEMOISELLE GIMEL

"So I am weak. Oh! yes, weak as all the rest. When I left Maclarey's at six sharp, I had nothing determined about me but my chin, which I carry a little high from habit. Raymonde called after me. I was already off; the street was as hot as a laundry room and my one thought was to walk the faster; I had no fear of being red when I should see him. That is a fear I have entertained at other times, when it was a question of presentations less serious. I had no fear of not pleasing; I was sure of being loved, loved forever, and my whole soul was strained only toward the words which should say that, and toward his glance, the only thing which made me afraid. I took the left side of the Avenue des Champs Elysées so as not to be opposite the greenhouse; I saw only the balustrade, white in the sunlight like a pen stroke, the trees above and black points moving slowly from one tree-trunk to the other. I wished for mamma's opera-glass. Carriages were returning from the Bois—many open hacks, some wedding landaus, some autos. No one has their heart as absorbed in one thought as mine; I wished for a balloon, to get in, to cross the square, and to light on the terrace saying: 'Here I am!'

"Well! Those were nearly my words to Monsieur Morand. My desire was so great to see him first, to come unawares upon him, thinking of me, that I took a way which seemed very simple to me and which he thought very clever when I told him about it. Where would Monsieur Morand, waiting for Mademoiselle Gimel coming from the Boulevard Malesherbes, place himself?

At the corner of the orange-house, near the Place de la Concorde, and he must look toward the west. I went around the orange-house then and arrived from the east, I followed the terrace above the quay. . . . And—quite at the end, motionless, leaning upon the balustrade, stood a young man, shielding his eyes with his right hand, placed as a visor on his forehead, searching with eagerness, with visible vexation, with knit eyebrows, the Place de la Concorde. I approached as softly as possible and said:

"'It is I, Monsieur, Evelyne Gimel.'

"I laughed, not to seem agitated. I dislike displaying my feelings. The three little nurse-maids, surrounded by children, saw me. I preferred that they should take me for an adventuress. He, too, was confused, on hearing my laugh. Oh! he did not tell me so. You easily pardon when you see for the first time face to face, alone, or nearly so, the one you love. He looked at me; and because he was very serious and agitated, his glance, which successively rested on my face, my laughing eyes, my cheeks which laughed and my smiling lips, did not know where to rest. Finally, he looked at my hands and said to me:

"'I thank you; I am very happy.'

"At that I gave him both my hands. And I laughed a little more softly, in answering:

"'Shall we walk?'

"The three little nurse-maids were looking at us with so lively an interest that I would have chosen to walk on the other side of the balustrade, on the square below, and I made a little move-

MADEMOISELLE GIMEL

ment to the left. But he opposed it, oh! gently, but very decidedly:

"'Straight ahead, if you please.'

"We passed in front of the bench, in the midst of the children. Immediately after, looking at me again, he said:

"'You laugh very readily, Mademoiselle.'

"'Oh! Monsieur, it is impossible to hide . . .'

"'I had already noticed that, and I shall seem very singular to you; I laugh at scarcely anything.'

"'And I at nearly everything.'

"'I hope you would not laugh, however, if a man should tell you that he loves you?'

"I was transported with joy at these words and grateful; but I do not know what stupid spirit of independence and of teasing, something not myself, triumphed over what is myself; I turned my head to the back of the island, the quays, and a little boat which was going up the Seine.

"'That depends on the man?'

"'If it were I?'

"I stopped. I threw my little decided glance, which still scoffed maliciously, full into his eyes: I saw that he was half wounded and I continued as if to wound him more:

"'Really, Monsieur, we scarcely know each other.'

"'It is true, Mademoiselle, you do not know me. I took the liberty of asking you to come, precisely to explain to you.'

"'And perhaps also to know who I am?'

"'Anything you would be willing to tell me of

yourself will give me pleasure but teach me little.'

"'Ah, indeed?'

"'I know you.'

"'Through Madame Mauléon, then?'

"'A little through her, but most of all through yourself. I have observed you during eleven breakfasts.'

"'What you have learned is at most a means of identification; but to become acquainted with each other takes longer!'

"'You are mistaken! a look is enough.' He said that with so much passion, quite at the end of the terrace near the Solferino bridge, that I was seized with a desire to thank him. But, as I am ashamed of demonstrations, as I think them weak, I looked incredulous.

"'No one has had such a look from me.'

"'You see very well that I know you, Mademoiselle; I was persuaded of it. You have never yet loved any one.'

"Well, I must confess that Monsieur Louis Morand is altogether nice! It was no use to reply to him with a joke and briefly. He was so willing to hear me, he did not tire of being amiable, of liking me and of telling me so. We glided, as the poets say, along the terrace in the glory of the sunset. No more nurses above, no more children; only people below the terrace, going home. I knew that mamma must be getting anxious, going to the window, repeating:

"'That darling is late coming home! Where is Evelyne? Half after six! six thirty-five even!'

"He told me all about himself. He was very unpretending, very modest—a little, probably, to be like me. I did not find him, however, familiar, which touched me deeply. Respect is almost a dream in our world. I did not appear astonished at this perfect politeness, of which he gave me the proof; but I lifted my eyes less frequently in his direction and I avoided doing so when he excused himself for not being rich, for not being able to give me, if I consented to become his wife, the luxury that he would have liked (these are his words) 'to place at my feet.' If our eyes had met, he would have seen too clearly in mine! He told me that he was born in the department of the Ain, in a pretty place called Linot, the one that he showed me on the postal card. His father, who was overseer of bridges and highways, is dead. And as I appeared to think that title very grand, without knowing what it was, he at once explained that I was mistaken; he was, I may say, obstinate, not knowing how to persuade me that he was of a very humble family. Truly, this Monsieur Morand does not resemble any of the young men whom I have known before; he does not flatter himself at all, he is afraid that you may think him better or richer than he is. He said:

"'We are quite poor, or rather I am able to live on condition that my mother makes little sacrifices; my pay is not enough and my mother makes it up. She is worthy of admiration. If you do me the honour to listen to me——'

"'But I am doing nothing else!'

"'Then, if you do me the honour to love me—'

Ah! with what decision he uttered that word, his head near mine and seeking my eyes, which were obstinately, unkindly looking at the distance, at the Arc de Triomphe! 'If you do me the honour to love me, I wish that you should know that you are not marrying a fortune. The army does not make one rich.'

"'Nor stenography either.'

"We began to laugh together, a long laugh, without speaking, he looking at me, I with my eyes fixed on the vague distance, but our two hearts so close to each other and so happy that I did not move lest it should end. A great wood pigeon, flying to rest, passed close to us and broke the charm. I was a little ashamed of my weakness; I asked:

"'You will not think the worse of me, Monsieur, if I am prudent? It is a quality that the life of a working girl would give to those even who might not have it naturally. You could choose a young girl who would bring you a fortune. Why choose a working girl? Why me?'

"We had resumed our walk and he made me no answer until we reached the Place de la Concorde. I had wounded him. He was ardent, rough, passionate, a little of the common people—I like that—in his way of revealing the blow. He told me that he had sworn to marry only a worthy woman, accustomed to work, clever in conquering life, and, at the same time, pretty, distinguished, able to play her part, make the regulation visits, quick-witted, self-possessed.

"'You are the one whom I was looking for,

Mademoiselle. Now, if I cannot please you, I prefer to know it at once; does my demand or my person appear perhaps ridiculous to you?—tell me?'

"I was agitated, I laughed no more, I answered:
"'I cannot judge of you in so short a time!'
"'Am I asking you to, Mademoiselle?'
"'Why, yes!'
"'Not at all; I only ask to see you again.'
"'Then, we are agreed. Will you come, to-morrow, to my mother's? She must be told.'
"'No.'
"'I cannot—however——'
"'Yes, you can put it off. I beg you to return here, to-morrow, to become better acquainted with me before consulting any other person, even your mother. Is that much to ask of you?'

"I looked at him a moment with all my eyes, with all my heart, with all my troubled good faith, and I found so much decision, loyalty and love in the depth of this look that I hesitated no longer.

"'Yes, Monsieur, it is much to ask of me. My mother is worthy of confidence. But I am willing to do this. I will not speak. I will return. Till to-morrow then!'

"I extended my hand to him gravely; I thought that he was going to kiss it. He pressed it lightly, respectfully, and I left him. I do not know how I still had the presence of mind to go down the flight of steps without stumbling, and across the Place. I divined his soul, I was wrapped in his thought, which he had thrown around me. And I felt a desire to brush the meshes away with my hand. I did not look back a single time, but I am certain that he remained there at the corner, by the side of the stairway, which serves as an entrance during the dog-show, until I disappeared by the rue Royale.

"Mamma was listening on the stairway to be quicker warned of my return. She almost cried out when she recognised my step and my hat. I called, going from one flight to the next, my head raised:

"'Poor mamma, we were kept at the bank.—Why do you worry?—The firm is about to make a large Peruvian loan, day after to-morrow.'

"'Plague take Peru!' She called from the top of the stairs. 'It has put me out of temper!'"

"Wednesday, July 17, ——.

"I have seen him again. When one meets for the first time, the emotion, the vastness of the unknown between two beings who have lived far from each other, the fear of being too trusting, —at least, with me—make the first meeting of those who think they love each other, a medley of effusion and of diplomacy, a little display, an uneasy search for permission to love, a sort of examination which one feels is too formidable to be thoroughly pleasant.

"You stake your heart, your repose, your dreams, you stake a family yet unborn and more than that. I had so vivid a sense of this peril, that we are in at the moment when we are going to give our love, that I restrained, all the time, not only my

MADEMOISELLE GIMEL 47

words but my heart, my smile even. That was very unlike me! I did not thank him when he told me things of which in my heart I was proud, because I was afraid of being forced the instant after to withdraw, to become again the little stenographer who is not easy to marry because her ambition is to marry a man 'of worth.'

"I begin to believe that he is really worthy. Our second interview was less long, but more confidential; we both of us felt less fear of being mistaken. I had on my white linen waist, which has a yoke of eyelet embroidery, and, through the cherry ribbon, knotted around my neck, I had slipped a sprig of mignonette. It is a delicate flower and faithful to the end; it dies, but it does not lose its leaves. Monsieur Morand saw the mignonette at once, because he looked at my small white throat and my shoulders, and he said to me:

"'The flower that I love best, precisely, Mademoiselle! At home, at our house at Valromey, my mother sows a bed of mignonette in a border every year, always the same, which perfumes the valley.'

"'Your valley is small then?'

"'No, very large. A little thing, a sprig of lavender or of mignonette, but which has a soul full of perfume, what power it has, and how far it goes!'

"'You are a poet?'

"'No, I am happy.'

"The nurses were all there on the bench. They laughed on seeing us again, and we laughed too.

It became embarrassing. I proposed to Monsieur Louis Morand that we should walk on the side of the terrace which goes along the Place de la Concorde. He assented. It is a great point to agree on the road. Immediately after, we became serious. Yes, both of us, and almost sad. During what seemed a long time, we ceased to be young and to feel that we were friends. Is it the same with everybody? Perhaps. We were like travellers who, reaching the port of embarkation, stop, less eager for the journey, full of questions about the sea, and the boat, and the wind. By and by, a step more, and there will be no longer time. We had both of us foreseen that moment, yet it had come suddenly. He questioned me about my childhood, my character, my tastes, and I asked him:

"'What would your mother say if you spoke of your plan to her, Monsieur? She might think that I did not belong to her world.'

"'She is the daughter of a very small proprietor.'

"'She was the wife of an overseer of bridges and highways.'

"'A very modest official! I guarantee you the consent of my mother, Mademoiselle, and more than that, her adoration.'

"I thanked him with a look, and I saw that he turned pale because of the tenderness of my look. This man, whose look is so stern, is very sensitive. I wished to know one thing, infinitely delicate, and I took advantage of his emotion.

"'The words which I guess, which I feel already

MADEMOISELLE GIMEL 49

upon your lips, are very fine; do not say them, however, Monsieur; I would like not to have any falsehood between us. Do not tell me yet that you love me. . . . I seem singular to you, perhaps?'

"'No; you surprise me, but deliciously.'

"'Then I may continue and question you with entire frankness?'

"'Yes.'

"'Even indiscreet? I would like to know one thing which you would have the right to conceal from me.'

"He knit his brows and took a moment or two to make his decision:

"'Continue just the same! I never lie.'

"'Very well! I would like to know if you have often said to other women the words which you would have said to me just now had I not stopped you?'

"'No, you are not the first to whom I have said "I love you"; I do not wish to make myself out better than I am; I swear to you, however, that I have not often been unfaithful to you, before I knew you, and that if we were married . . .'

"'What do you know about it?'

"'I answer for it, I will be the friend who does not change. I have the habit of obeying orders; and then, with you it would be easy.'

"'Easy? I have not seen many plays, Monsieur, but none said that. Still, I believe you.— I need to believe you.'

"He left these words unanswered, and we walked without speaking side by side for the space of four trees at least. I am persuaded that he was sincere. When men are young and are near us, they are very sure of themselves. Then, he asked me two questions more:

"'Would you be willing to leave Paris?'

"'It would be very hard for me; I love it.'

"'Impossible?'

"'No, because I am capable of loving some one more than I love my Paris; I am sure of that.'

"Then, imperiously, without change, as if he were making a speech to his men, he said to me:

"'I am a soldier; but I am ignorant of everything else. A short time at college, then early in the troop, then to Saint-Maixent. You understand that I have few ties. I own to you that I am not well grounded in religion. But I ask nothing better than to learn of you, because I have comrades, whom I esteem greatly, those whom I esteem the most, who are fervent believers. My mother is a devout Christian. What is your belief on the subject?'

"I was forced to reply. I was content that he should be better than I, who have not his excuses and who am an indifferent observer of religious duties. Excuses, why yes, I may have some perhaps, thinking carefully . . . mamma, for instance, is not at all devout; my life as a clerk, which is not surrounded by many examples. . . . I promised to instruct Monsieur Louis Morand. But it will be necessary first to instruct the teacher, who is not of the first order. I cannot tell how happy this frank talk, without the shadow of hypocrisy on either side, made me. My great Paris had become almost silent—you can never ask complete silence of it. The air from the Bois came so soft that I felt myself affected breathing it. Monsieur Morand sometimes followed with his eye the rosy clouds and smiled at them. I found this dangerous for a certain little Evelyne Gimel, who will have no real advice in this serious affair, and who has much trouble already to make herself take forty-eight hours' reflection. I broke this melancholy of love which was seizing us both. I asked:

"'Where did you drill this morning, Monsieur?'

"'At Issy-les-Molineaux.'

"'Do you mean Issy-les-Aéroplanes?'

"'Precisely. I have witnessed two flights. '

"'How I should have loved to be there! It is my passion! Every day I buy a paper to know when we will fly. Who was it? Delagrange? Malécot? Ferber? The lady aviator?'

"'None of them, but new ones, some quite young men, who threw themselves into the air, borne aloft by very fine linen wings that looked like those of a butterfly.'

"'Tell me about it!'

"'I would rather tell you to-morrow.'

"His expression was so serious that I felt that my laugh rang false. There was so much true love in his eyes that I said yes. I promised to come back again, for the last time."

"Thursday, July 18, ——.

"It is the third evening of my love. Alas, the last of my joy! All is over. I write this at I do not know what hour of the night, while Madame

Gimel—I must call her so now—weeps too and suffers almost as much as I.

"My love began so well! This very evening at ten minutes after six, he was waiting for me upon the terrace that we had chosen for our meetings, and he had, like myself, a whole rising tide of thoughts in his heart. I had not confessed that I was beginning to love him; I was going to tell it to him; I was no longer afraid of him. On leaving the bank, I looked up at the sky and I received a drop of water on my cheek. Any other day, every day, I would have been furious, for I was without an umbrella; but now, I stretched out my ten fingers, tired with striking the keys of my machine, and I said, I remember:

"'I will get there rumpled, if I must, but that makes no difference to me; he loves me now, and I am going to tell him that I love him.'

"Why? That is the secret of yesterday's words, words which are seeds, which shoot up their first two leaves in a night. And I did not take a roundabout way going to the rendezvous; no, I went straight ahead, under the drizzling rain which was falling and whose drops I would have been willing for him to drink from my cheek. He was at the lookout; I saw his tall silhouette in the distance, above the white balustrade, between two trunks of trees; and then, I saw his motionless face. We were drawn by each other, and I alone was advancing; I saw his eyes which were full of me; I went up the steps, no one was there but ourselves; I ran and I said:

"'I love you!'

MADEMOISELLE GIMEL

"Then, oh! then his eyes filled suddenly with tears. And he weeping, I nearly, we were infinitely happy under the rain, in those deserted Tuileries. I think that we walked very softly, but I am not sure. In our hearts we were betrothed. He looked at me for a long time without speaking, his firm eyes, his eyes of command and of justice, fixed on mine, and I saw, trembling on the corner of his lips, the words of love which he was too agitated to utter. He had become dumb.

"'I understand it all, Monsieur, but it is raining. Let us go in.'

"But where? The great conservatory of the Tuileries was there, all its glass windows wide open, showing the palms, the orange-trees, bananas, ferns, and guarded only by a little iron chain festooned from one post to the other. Well, we entered; I stood leaning against a box and Monsieur Morand was leaning against the same one. It was a very large box; we stood under the orange-tree, and I do not know whether that brings luck, but I shall never live moments more sweet. He was looking before him at the falling rain and I was doing the same; I believe indeed that we saw nothing but the future, of which we did not speak. He had taken my hand and he pressed it often, and even in the interval I felt it small, trusting, loved, between his strong fingers, which trembled too. . . . What did he say to me? Nothing of any moment! It was a kind of plaint, which seemed to me delicious and which he called 'telling of his youth.'

"'I have suffered,' he repeated, 'until the moment when I knew you. My life has been poor and lonely and, at last you are here!'

"What happiness there was for me and for him in this past sadness! I pitied him. I had the feeling that I was beginning my rôle as a woman, which is to console. He talked nonsense, and I too, in the hope that it might last. We allowed long silences to fall between the words; but they were filled with a kind of loving pity which he asked for and which I gave. There is a language, from soul to soul, which has no words; it is like a changeable colour enveloping us. Contrary to my custom, I was not gay. I did not find again what has been my way of being happy up to the present time. I wished for nothing except to hear him say continually:

"'I have suffered, and at last you are here!'

"Suddenly a door in the rear of the greenhouse opened; a gardener entered from back of the palms.

"'Upon my word! Lovers! Not shy either! Will you clear out! The conservatory of the Tuileries is not a marquise restaurant!'

"Monsieur Louis Morand is a man of self-possession; I saw that at once. He drew himself up; he looked at the gardener, who was approaching, and when he was near he said calmly:

"'Your name is Jean Jules Plot, you were corporal three years ago in the 3rd of the 2nd. Were you not?'

"'That is possible. And you?'

"'Lieutenant Louis Morand. You were not in my company. But I recognised you.'

"'It is because you are in citizen's dress, Lieutenant; I beg pardon.'

"With that, they moved away, and I heard the gardener say in a low tone:

"'My compliments, Lieutenant; she is altogether *chic*, your lady-love.'

"'Say my fiancée, Jean Jules Plot.'

"Turning he looked at me. Ah! the beautiful frank eyes in which there was love enough for a whole life and even for two! The rain had nearly stopped; I made a sign:

"'Shall we go out?'

"He opened his umbrella, I took my place quite near my 'fiancé'; he was so happy that I could have led him to the right, to the left, no matter where.

"'I love you, Mademoiselle Evelyne.'

"We walked down the garden slope, we passed by the side of the fountain, near old father Nile, buried under the mass of his children; we passed between the bars.

"'Mademoiselle Evelyne, I love—but where are we going?' he asked.

"'To see my mother! It is time to tell her, after three rendezvous!'

"I do not know whether he rightly understood, for, from the Tuileries to the rue Saint-Honoré, his only thought apparently was of me, he did not speak of her.

"Never have I mounted the stairs of our house more slowly. Ah! how right I was! Happiness, it is joy which believes that it is going to last. Mine was not entirely complete. It trembled a little. What was mamma going to say? But I knew her weakness for me. Monsieur Morand on the first step had taken my arm and had placed it in his.

"'Are there but four stories?' said he. 'What a pity! I would appreciate an American sky-scraper at this time!'

"I was of the same mind. It was light still in the great white cage. No one disturbed our ascent. When we reached the top we had the same beating of the heart, the same recoil before the copper button of the bell. Behind the door, what word was going to be spoken! What fate was lying in wait for us? I reached out my hand very slowly. Monsieur Morand saw the movement, and, it may be in order to put off the moment when we should be there, he took my hand and carried it to his lips, and I felt them praying on my fingers and saying:

"'Not yet.'

"That lasted a little. I believe that I would have let the prayer continue had I not heard mamma's step. She was coming, probably, to lean over the balustrade. It was Monsieur Morand who rang. Then he stood back and mamma came hastily, joyously to open the door, as she did every evening. She saw me first; I saw the smile, which welcomes me and which belongs to me, begin; but suddenly, it ceased. Mamma had just discovered this young man behind me; her near-sighted eyes made an effort, she wrinkled her eyelids, she asked herself:

"'Do I know him?'

"She made the little movement of the head which precedes the salutation. But no, she does not know this gentleman. He is a stranger, she does not understand; she remembers that she still has on her black alpaca apron and I see her draw back her poor, troubled, dull, pinched face into the shadow of the passage, while I go forward and say very low:

"'Mamma, I will explain to you. Do not be afraid of anything. Let us go into the sitting-room.'

"Her first movement on entering the room, which is hers, was to throw the surprised apron under the sewing-machine. Then she seemed to recover her presence of mind; she turned the lamp up:

"'Please come in, Monsieur. What is the matter? - I was not expecting a call. If you will close the window, Evelyne?'

"When she was seated with her back to the light, when the window was closed, mamma had already regained her usual sure air, her Parisian air.

"'But please be seated, Monsieur.'

"She looked at him, during this time. She studied him. She classified him. I was on her left, by the armchair, and much more agitated than at the Tuileries. I looked at him too, and I thought him wonderful and charming.

"He was not embarrassed, not awkward nor gawky; he was agitated; and, what struck me as very proper and very clever, he only looked at mamma regardless of all the rest of the room.

He waited with deference for her to act, he waited without impatience until he could say what he wished to say. He remained standing; and it was very simple. I had not had time to explain anything. He took the explanations on himself.

"'Madame,' he said, 'I should have spoken to you day before yesterday. It is already three days since I made my declaration to Mademoiselle Evelyne.'

"She put on her expression of astonishment, an expression that she had seen assumed in plays, happy really, poor mamma, very happy.

"'What kind of a declaration, Monsieur?'

"I was so close to her that I bent forward, and kissing her where her white hairs began, I said:

"'Of love, Mamma.'

"And in a lower tone:

"'It happened quite properly. . . . At the Tuileries. . . . He is very gentlemanly. . . . Receive him well.'

"He did not speak. She gazed at him for perhaps half a moment. She is sensitive, impressionable! I read everything in her face; she was asking herself:

"'Let me see, does that countenance impress me? Would he have pleased me when I was young, when I was saleswoman at Revillon's? Let me see, the mustache, the eyebrows a little rough, this calm and stubborn brow, these eyes of command, but which love, which have some fear too, not of me, but of what I am going to say.—Yes, surely, Evelyne has done what I would have done. . . . Although, yes, certainly, Monsieur Gimel, adjutant of the Republican Guard, was a handsomer man.'

"'Excuse me, Monsieur; one is not prepared for such news. I am overcome. Tell me how you became acquainted with Evelyne? Are you in her bank?'

"He began to laugh, and I can still hear this restrained but frank laugh, the last between us.

"'Oh no, Madame! No! I began by two years in the Soudan.'

"'Gracious! You live in the colonies?'

"'I lived there yesterday; I would willingly return there, if I had not the place which I have just confessed to you. I am a lieutenant of infantry.'

"Mamma suddenly became very pale, she was at a loss for words, she, who is always so ready and so quick!

"'An officer! But, Monsieur, a regulation dot is necessary; I do not know whether Evelyne, even after my death . . .'

"'No, Mamma, it is not necessary any more! I made that objection myself, you recall, Monsieur, by the side of the myrtle tree as the gardener came in. I had just asked you. . . . No, Mamma, there is a circular of the general . . .'

"I thought that mamma was going to smile. No, she became still more pale; she looked as if she were going to faint; she looked at us in turn with a kind of stupor, as if one or the other of us were going to die.

"'Really, Monsieur,' she said, 'this project is

impossible—utterly impossible.—The honour was great, without doubt—but Evelyne cannot marry an officer. Will you wait for me here? I have something to say to the child, who does not understand, more than you, what I wish to say. Come, my child.'

"Saying that, she drew me into my room. I was not afraid; I felt myself strong against all opposition, capable of waiting, of exiling myself, of continuing to work, of learning a new trade if it were necessary, of so many things that I was sure that whatever argument mamma was going to oppose would not hold out against my will. Could I have foreseen? Ah! I was too confident! A word sufficed to crush me! She drew me to the window; she passed her arm around my waist; she hid her face from me; she spoke to me her forehead resting on my hair. At once, I felt my poor love struck with death; I did not defend myself; I did not answer; I suffered. How long did I remain there, without strength, while she urged me:

"'Come, my child, go back, invent a pretext, send him away, since it must be done!'

"Seeing that I remained silent, she even proposed to me to go alone and to say herself to Monsieur Morand:

"'It is ended, do not return.'

"Then only I came to myself. I repulsed her; she let me act. My nerves were tense, therefore fortified. I must have looked very strange, my eyes glittering with the tears that I was holding back; with my new will to leave him; with my

MADEMOISELLE GIMEL 61

voice which I was afraid of hearing myself, because it was going to separate us. I do not know how I had the courage, I went straight to him, standing in the middle of the room.

"'Monsieur, there is a great sorrow for me and for you; Madame Gimel has just told me. I was ignorant of what she has told me, I swear it to you. She was right to tell me, I must not, I can not be your fiancée.'

"'But what can she have told you, Mademoiselle? She does not know me. Someone, perhaps, has slandered me to her? Let her make inquiries. I have nothing to fear. But do not say such words.'

"'Oh! no, it is nothing about you.'

"'Then, how can a thing which you did not know, and which concerned you, Mademoiselle, have so great importance? You were ignorant of it—what is it? Have I not assured you that questions of dot did not enter into my thoughts. If you were without anything and without trousseau, I should not change my mind. Is that all?'

"'Alas! no.'

"'Then speak, tell me!'

"'I cannot.'

"'You must! I will not leave you without knowing why you break off. I have the right to an explanation.'

"'And if I ask you, Monsieur, not to demand it?'

"'I refuse.—You see that I suffer cruelly. I shall believe that I have been rejected for reasons of ambition, which you have been made to share.'

"'Indeed, no! Do not insult the child, Monsieur! She had the right to choose, in fact she had chosen, and she is not the woman to take back her word from ambition!'

"It was Madame Gimel, who came out, in her turn, from my room, animated, flushed, ready to take offence for me, who was only unhappy. I reached out my hand to stay the pleadings of this loving, offended one; I said:

"'You are right, Monsieur, it is better that you should know the truth.'

"'What, you are going to tell him, Evelyne?'

"'Everything; Monsieur Morand will see by that how greatly I esteem him. He will also see that I cannot become his wife.—I am a foundling, Monsieur, I am a ward of Public Charity, adopted by Madame Gimel. Do you understand now? This woman, who has brought me up, had only to leave me with the others. I should have grown up on a farm in Nièvre or in Normandy. I am without father or mother. You yourself see that I am not one who can be presented to the wives of officers. You cannot deny it.'

"He looked at me, and he loved me still. But he did not reply. He saw that I was not lying, that I had been ignorant of everything, that I did not wish to weep, that I did not wish him to remain. He too wished to be courageous; he did not even ask me to take his hand; he bowed to mamma, the poor boy, bewildered and yet correct; he bowed to her and then he did not have

MADEMOISELLE GIMEL 63

the strength to bid me farewell. I think that he tried to begin: 'Pardon me—' but he had not the courage to finish, he felt that everything was crumbling to pieces, and he left the room. I am almost sure that he stopped to look at me on the landing. I did not move. The ward of Public Charity had no word of hope to give him, no illusion. The dry click of the lock, resuming its rôle of guardian, has separated us.

"Madame Gimel spoke:

"'Come, let me tell you everything!'

"We talked and wept until two o'clock in the morning. And, now, I have no father, no mother, no name of my own, and no longer a fiancé."

III.

NUMBER 149,007.

At eight o'clock Evelyne was up. She had made her bed, swept the room, and had heated the milk which the milkman, at half past seven every morning, placed upon the door-mat in a sealed bottle with a blue label: "Select milk from the Château de Perray."

She carried the two cups on a tray into the room of Madame Gimel.

"Thank you, my dear. Do not hurry. You have plenty of time. There, put the tray on the stand. Go get the rolls. That is all. Why have you put on a black dress and your black tie? You look——"

"As if I were in mourning? That is what I wish."

"Yes, my poor darling. But what will the others at the bank say?"

"I am not going there."

"How! You are not going there?"

"No, we are going, both of us, on an urgent errand, and I will send a note to Monsieur Amédée, to say that I am ill."

"If they learn that it is not true?"

"It is truer than if the doctor had said so——"

"That is true. And where do you want——"

"To the Bureau of Public Charity. I am going to ask for my mother. I wish to know her name, who she is, and to find her again if she is not dead."

"You will learn nothing, my child, since I have known nothing."

"Because you are timid! Because you are from Romorantin, while I—I am a Parisienne— Though as to that, I am no longer sure of anything! But I assure you that they will tell it to me!"

She had the appearance of a very young widow who was beside herself.

"Yes, dearest, they will tell it perhaps. You are right. Drink your milk. I will put on my hat. Sit down. There, don't hurry. We have plenty of time. I am always your mother, my Evelyne."

The pale Madame Gimel took more time than usual to pin on her hat. Like others, when they have aged a little, she sought for words to console

MADEMOISELLE GIMEL 65

the sorrow of love, which had no wish to be consoled and which burst into brighter flame at the useless words. Evelyne, seated facing the light, near the little table, looked into space above the opposite roofs, which were visible through the open window, and forgot to touch the bowl of milk which sent up trembling wreaths of steam.

Behind her, Madame Gimel, dressed for the walk, having even taken her "best" parasol, which had a cherry on the end of the handle, stood erect for a little time. She pitied Evelyne; she envied her, perhaps; she turned over in her mind the incidents of this living romance which was under her eyes, as she did in her hours of solitude, when she had finished a continued story in the *Petit Journal*. But this time, she ran against the unknown and the impossible on all sides. "I am ready, my child; I am waiting for you."

Evelyne swallowed a mouthful of milk and went out first.

While the two women were walking in the street their eyes and even their hearts were distracted a little. It was still early. They followed the rue de Rivoli, which they had entered, leaving the rue Saint-Honoré. Madame Gimel had chosen this route on purpose to pass under the galleries of the Louvre shops, to be able to speak the words which have power over the minds of women—she knew them well—which appeal where there is love of self, of another, or of child.

"Look at that beautiful guipure bertha; and this dress for the seashore! And that adorable layette!"

In spite of her grief, Evelyne looked. She did not go so far as to smile, but a little caress came to her from things exposed in the window that struck her fancy. Her heart was not wholly closed to life, but almost so. She had on her black skirt, a flexible leather belt, a white waist and her everyday sailor hat from which a pigeon's wing rose, a single one.

When Madame Gimel turned to the right, a little before reaching the Hôtel de Ville, quite two minutes had passed without her speaking. Old memories and the dread of those offices, behind which the State sits, threw a gloom over her. Evelyne, the impressionable Evelyne, haughty because ashamed, hostile beforehand to all that she was going to see and to hear, hesitated, her head raised, between the façades of the public buildings which occupy nearly the whole length of Victoria Avenue.

"It is at No. 3, the Public Relief," said Madame Gimel. "I remember you have to go in the court. Ah! dear me! I was so happy twenty-two years ago when I came out of there with you in my arms, and my good husband, worthy soul, who was murmuring behind me: 'You don't know how to carry her right, give her to me.' This brings back so many things. There was a clerk—but what am I saying?—there were several chiefs of bureaus and the director who made us sign papers that day. I might, perhaps, recognise some of them."

The memory of the heart is not that of the eyes. Madame Gimel, on entering the court of

MADEMOISELLE GIMEL 67

No. 3, took her lorgnette and looked, unable to decide, at the flights of steps and the doors around the court, when Evelyne went to the right, to the glass door upon which were inscribed these words: "Foundlings.—Information and Inquiries." The two women entered, turned to the left, and passed before an office where the examiners of the suburbs of Paris were holding forth, giving the accounts of their researches. They came to a little window like that of a bank, behind which a fat, grave, smooth-shaven man was standing, who had expressive lips and who knew it. He did not move on seeing Madame Gimel and Evelyne. The latter did not advance. Madame Gimel glided lightly, with the step she had had at Revillon's when advancing to meet a customer, and said:

"Monsieur, the Chief of the Bureau?"

He answered immediately:

"Have you the child's number?"

"No, Monsieur, I haven't it with me, but I remember it perfectly: 149,007."

The clerk turned to an inclined desk upon which a register lay. Madame Gimel saw plainly that he was in error, but she did not dare tell him so, on account of the reverential fear with which every official inspired her. The clerk crushed under his thumb and turned with a swift, circular motion five or six leaves, then let them drop again.

"Why," he exclaimed, "this is No. 170,000! Your number is old, Madame."

A firm, young voice spoke:

"Monsieur, I am No. 149,007!"

The fat scribe was struck with the accent of this voice, and when he looked at Evelyne, who had advanced to Madame Gimel's right, his astonishment became admiration. The expressive lips made a sign.

"Pardon me, Mademoiselle; I could not suspect——"

"That does not matter," interrupted the young girl. "I was adopted twenty-two years ago by Madame——"

"Oh! Evelyne!"

"Naturally. How would you have me explain? I have come, Monsieur, to get some information about my origin."

She was nervous and decided to be impertinent.

The head of the bureau saw that. He economised the rest of the smile, which was waiting its turn, and answered:

"Very well, Mademoiselle. Apply then to the Bureau of Adoptions, stairway A, top floor."

He bowed with administrative politeness, yet with a shade of reserve, on account of the abruptness of the young girl. Madame Gimel alone acknowledged it. The pigeon-wing had already flitted on and passed in front of the examiners, who blinked their eyes in Evelyne's wake.

The latter, recrossing the court, found stairway A, mounted several flights, and went down a corridor upon which numbered doors opened. She knocked at one of the last, and entered a warm cell of a room whose occupant her knock had awakened.

"I do not remember him either," whispered Madame Gimel, coming close to Evelyne.

The man pushed forward two chairs, the only ones which furnished the room. He belonged to that intelligent and ardent class who rush into public office, who invent and meditate on reforms, make reports, hope for advancement, and, receiving very little, sometimes get angry, but more often relax their vigilance. His ample forehead, which the baldness of his temples prolonged, and his pointed chin with its curved beard, gave him a triangular head. He glanced at the little red curtains which framed the window, at the Empire clock, two black columns and a gold dial, at the files of papers lined up before him, to assure himself that all was in order, placed a small eyeglass on his nose, which was also triangular, and asked:

"What can I do for you, Madame?"

Evelyne did not give Madame Gimel time to reply.

"It appears, Monsieur," said she, "that I am No. 149,007. I learned yesterday evening that I was not the daughter of Madame Gimel; that I was a ward of the Public Relief. I have come to ask you to tell me my mother's name, to permit me to find her again, if she is living.—I am extremely unhappy.—Especially, I beg of you—no consolations and no commonplaces."

Monsieur Heidemetz gave an approving glance and replied:

"That does not seem to me possible. You or Madame must have———"

"Gimel, Monsieur; my husband was adjutant in the Republican Guard."

"Madame Gimel should have a certificate of origin, guaranteed by the Administration."

"Yes, I have seen it; it is a document which shows nothing. You cannot admit that a child may be abandoned without the mother giving her name?"

"I beg your pardon, but that is so, Mademoiselle."

"Without her making known what motive has actuated her?"

"That may happen, on the contrary."

"From whence one springs, from what poverty or from what vice? For I can only hesitate between those two things."

"Come, come, my little Evelyne, calm yourself."

"Let me alone; I am speaking to monsieur, who sees that I wish to know all that he knows himself, and I think that my pretension is not excessive——"

The hand of Monsieur Heidemetz removed the eye-glass and seemed to fondle it.

"It is, Mademoiselle. You have a right only to the information contained in the Administration's certificate of origin. Nevertheless, to oblige you, I am going to do an exceptional thing, altogether exceptional, one which I have vainly asked should be made obligatory on the Public Relief."

He rang for a messenger.

"Go, ask for this file at the archives." He wrote two lines upon a slip of paper, which he

MADEMOISELLE GIMEL 71

handed to the messenger, and immediately began to question Madame Gimel about the circumstances of what he termed: "The placing under guardianship." Madame Gimel recalled with complaisance the long discussions that she had had with Monsieur Gimel before deciding to adopt a child; the indecision of her husband, who did not know whether he would adopt a boy or girl; her own insistence in asking for "a little girl"; the comparison of the photographs of the "candidates"; then the coming of the couple, accompanied by a notary, to the director of the Public Relief himself, "in that fine office where the portraits of benevolent persons of all ages are hung."

Evelyne did not speak, in spite of the attentions of the young clerk, who furnished her with explanations which she did not ask for.

When the messenger returned, she rose and went quickly to the table on which he placed a small yellow file of papers.

"Ah! Let me see."

"Look."

Evelyne bent forward, her hands resting on the table. She followed the text which Monsieur Heidemetz read rapidly in an undertone. It was a double cream-coloured sheet of large size, having on each leaf, on the first page and on the reverse, a printed list of questions, with square spaces opposite, nearly all empty, alas!

"Bulletin of information concerning a child presented at the Foundling Hospital. Sex of child: feminine. Name and surname: Evelyne."

"Then I have no other name, Monsieur?"

"Evelyne, nothing more, Mademoiselle. You can see. Place and date of birth, Department: Paris, October 1, 1886."

"At least I was born in Paris," said Evelyne.

"Is it legitimate or illegitimate? Illegitimate. Recognised by the father? No. By the mother? No. Place of confinement? Blank. Wish of the parents as to creed? Blank."

"Ah! as for that, she was baptised, Monsieur," interrupted Madame Gimel. "I took care to have her baptised conditionally, as they say. And I may even add that she is very religious for a— That is, I mean to say; I have brought her up as my own child."

"Date of deposit. You were twelve days old, Mademoiselle. Detailed explanation of the motives which led to the abandonment of the child."

Here monsieur showed a delicate attention. He had a feeling that the young creature who was standing near him suffered, and he did not read aloud the motive written in the space for the answers; the motive in a single word: poverty. Evelyne was grateful to him for this. He turned the page. The mother had been unwilling to give any information about herself which could identify her, and all that she had consented to say was that she had had no other child but the one which she abandoned.

The third page must have been the hardest for Evelyne, and the silence was complete while Evelyne read these cruel lines:

"Has the mother been told that the admission

MADEMOISELLE GIMEL

of a child to the Foundling Hospital did not constitute a temporary placing, but an effective abandonment?" "Yes."

"And that the consequences were the following: absolute ignorance of the places where the infant would be put to nurse or be placed?" "Yes."

"Absence of all communication, even indirect, with it?" "Yes."

The young girl turned her head aside an instant to Madame Gimel.

"My mother must have been very unhappy," she said, "to accept that!"

Madame Gimel's eyes were red, and she could not reply. Evelyne read this last condition:

"News of the child given every three months only, and confined merely to the question of existence or of decease?"

And there was again "Yes" in the column of replies.

Monsieur Heidemetz folded the leaf, and the noise of rustling paper ran from one wall to the other and reigned alone during some seconds in this mansard above that great world Paris, where three persons were living over again a story twenty-two years old. Evelyne asked very low:

"Is that all that I shall know of her?"

"It is all that we know, Mademoiselle."

"She never came to ask for news of her child, afterward?"

"I do not know; it would be necessary to make researches; to oblige you, I can——"

"No, I thank you."

She stepped back; the chief of the bureau

turned the leaves of file 149,007, partly to satisfy his sense of duty, partly to hide his emotion.

"Ah! Let me see that, Monsieur; I think I remember——"

Madame Gimel had seen a note, between a report and the black-covered register of Evelyne, sent by the agent of Bourbon l'Archambault; she seized and read it, to console Evelyne—to console herself.

"Listen, my dear, how pretty you were then already. This is what decided Monsieur Gimel and me. Oh! how we weighed each word: 'Two candidates appear to me to have different chances to be proposed with a view to adoption: No. 149,007. A beautiful child, blonde, strong for her age.'" She was beaming. Evelyne behind her said:

"Let us go, if you don't mind. Good-bye, Monsieur."

"Mademoiselle!"

She felt that he remained in the opening of the door on the threshold and that he was following with his glance this abandoned one, who would suffer all her life for the fault of an unknown woman. Poor Evelyne, the smiling one! At least, no one had seen her weep; she would not weep; she walked very rapidly to avoid the questions of the one who had adopted her, who trotted behind her. Two nurses, a clerk of the hospital and three silly girls on the stairway stepped aside and were silent a moment to allow this sorrow to pass. One of the women remarked:

"Why is she in half-mourning? Her grief must

be very recent. Her face is all drawn by suffering!"

Madame Gimel had also her share in this grief. She suffered most of all from this diminution of tenderness and respect which she remarked since the evening before in the young girl.

"You try to act the part of a mother," she thought, "you love with a love equal to a mother's love, but devotion counts but little with children whom you have only loved; it is necessary to give them birth."

The conversation on the street was limited to words exchanged in haste:

"Take care of the auto."

"I see it."

"It is going to rain!"

"Probably."

"A storm."

"Yes."

Evelyne and Madame Gimel going down Victoria Avenue, took, to return home and without paying any attention, the quai of the Mégisserie, and the quai of the Louvre. There, as Evelyne turned obliquely to the right:

"Do you want to go back by the rue de Rivoli? It is cooler here."

"No, I am going to Saint-Germain-l'Auxerrois."

Madame Gimel was amazed and she was still more so when she saw Evelyne ask an employee of the church if the attending priest was there, when she followed her into the sacristy and heard the following conversation:

"Monsieur l'Abbé, can you have a mass said for a woman whom you have not known, whose name you do not even know, nothing about her, nothing?"

"Certainly, Mademoiselle; it is enough that she has existed and that your thought attributes the merit to her."

"Then, I beg you to say a mass for my unknown mother."

"Very well, Mademoiselle. Do you wish it on any fixed day?"

"No."

She handed the abbé three francs, who said:

"But it is not so much, Mademoiselle."

Evelyne had already left the sacristy. At the door she stopped upon the steps before the grating and, when she felt that the maternal shadow had rejoined her, she said:

"Mamma"—Madame Gimel found the return of that word sweet—"Mamma, I ask your pardon if I have wounded, pained, astonished you. I have not quite had my heart nor my brain since yesterday. I will recover them, but I only ask of you one thing—not to pity me. That would lessen my courage. And do not even ask me what I am thinking of. . . ."

Madame Gimel kissed her, standing there on the steps, and that was her answer, her way of taking an oath.

IV.

THE DRILL AT BAGATELLE.

Three companies of infantry were drilling at six o'clock in the morning, on the 12th of August, on the turf of Bagatelle.

They were not in full strength, and one of the three spectators following the evolutions of the troops—I speak only of manifest witnesses—had just counted, in all, one hundred and fifty-three men, jotting down this figure in a note-book in the midst of abbreviated memoranda. It was Colonel Ridault. The two other observers, who did not take notes, were two Apaches, lying at the end of the turf, their legs doubled up, their linen sandals waving at the end of their balanced feet.

The colonel, coming without being expected or invited, left his horse on the road, taking his stand by the side of the avenue leading to the château. Standing and front view, he had still a fine military figure; in profile, you saw the circumflex accent too much. He was growing stout and he deplored the fact.

But he did nothing to prevent it and continued to dine often in town. He was much sought after. Colonel Ridault supported the government and suffered from it only in what he called "his line." He knew that his opinions, especially those that were attributed to him, were a hindrance to his career. Just what were the opinions of Colonel Ridault? He would have been embarrassed to have told. Endowed with a spirit of contradiction, which he had not exercised without losing something of his best-reasoned and most cherished ideas, it might be said that he had only one conviction, only one passion, only one idea which he himself never criticised: the army. This injured him with the civilian officials who disposed of grades. He was too much a soldier in a time when they did not fight. This old bachelor, who showed but a discreet sympathy for the trials of people of the world, became paternal, ridiculously tender at times, when it concerned one of his officers or one of his soldiers. His pay was dissipated in loans, that is to say, in gifts. The head round, moustache straight, grey, and fair, eyes blue, chin always a little raised, Colonel Ridault never laughed in uniform. He permitted himself to joke only in the evening, judging that that was, like the good dinner, the repose of a strong man. Long ago people had said of him: "There goes a future great general." Now they said: "Eighteen juniors have been promoted over his head! In fifteen months, he will be retired as a colonel. It is ended." Colonel Ridault had more difficulty than public opinion in accepting the situation. However, he began to make his plans known, among his friends, for this approaching period. With no relatives, except some distant cousins, with whom he had quarrelled on hunting questions, the colonel would retire to a country house in the south, near Villefranche, and there he would be able to economise

MADEMOISELLE GIMEL 79

enough to enable him to pass the three beautiful spring months in Paris. "In the meantime," said he, "I shall continue the task of my life, which is to enforce discipline."

The colonel inspected the three companies attentively for ten minutes, when, taking advantage of an interval of repose, he called:

"Lieutenant Morand?"

The lieutenant stepped out from a group of officers and non-commissioned officers and came double-quick time, holding his sabre in his left hand. It was soon done, he jumped from the turf on the sand of the path, and took the position of the inferior before the superior.

"You are acting as captain of the company?"

"Yes, Colonel, I am the ranking officer."

"How many men are there?"

"Forty-eight in my company; one hundred and fifty-one in the three."

"That is an error; I counted one hundred and fifty-three; you have some on sick report?"

"Five in all, Colonel; but the garrison duty, the fatigue duty, the officers——"

"Tricks also, isn't it so? You will send me, as soon as you have returned, the total strength, present and absent."

The lieutenant gave a sign of assent. The colonel reached out his hand to him then:

"Monsieur Morand, you have not been losing at cards?"

The serious face of the lieutenant relaxed for a second.

"No, Colonel."

"You have no difficulties with your superior officers?"

"None."

"Nothing in the profession which frets you?"

"Nothing."

"You are lucky! All the same you have your troubles, that is plain; everybody remarks it; your captain told me that you no longer spoke a word outside of the service. I know that troubles not connected with the service are none of my business; I have no remedy for them, unless the friendship of an old man may be of some use—and that rarely happens."

Morand, who had great powers of self-control, did not let, at first, anything of what he thought appear. Then his guarded eyes became softer; something, an icy barrier of hardness and of reserve, fell away.

"I have indeed, a counsel that I would like to ask of you, my Colonel."

"Continue, my dear fellow."

He made a sign to the officers, who were looking on, a hundred paces distant on the turf, to continue the drill; and he began walking on the gravel of the still deserted path, on the right of the lieutenant, who spoke, his eyes fixed on the distant horizon. They walked some hundred paces from north to south, faced about, and then began again. Second Lieutenant Léguillé, Adjutant Pratt, and Lieutenant Roy, from the distance, said to each other: "He is a lucky fellow, that Morand! And the worst of it is that he will not tell us a thing. We shall never know whether the colonel has confided the secret of the mobilisation to him, or inquired about his grandfather!"

Colonel Ridault did not speak, did not ask a question: he listened. Neither of them made gestures. An attentive observer might have noted a certain resemblance of bearing and gait between this young, slender man and this other, who had grown stout, but was yet capable of feeling enthusiasm and especially that impulse which made sometimes the one, sometimes the other, raise his head, leading them to seek points on the horizon where sad eyes might wander without danger of tears or of betrayal. Monsieur Ridault scarcely spoke, or did so merely to start Morand with a phrase like: "And after?" "And what does your mother think?" Oftenest, he only uttered an encouraging monosyllable: "Good!"

Morand finished and waited for the judgment as if he had been before a council of war. Nothing came. The words stuck in the colonel's throat and choked him.

"I repeat my question, Colonel: is it not your opinion that there is nothing to be done, that I would never succeed in having a foundling admitted into the society of the regiment?"

"No, nothing to be done, except what you have done. I am sorry for you. Give me your hand. And renew your betrothal with the army. Au revoir!"

V.

THE 12TH OF AUGUST.

Evelyne was as good as her word; she did not weep; she never alluded to the hard blow which had struck her youth; she did not even complain of life in vague terms, so as not to enter, by that wide road, into the paths to which we all return so willingly to wound ourselves on the same stones and the same thorns. Something had died in her, her gaiety; in spite of her resolute will, Evelyne did not laugh any more.

Her two associates at Maclarey's bank had noticed this from the first day, but they had not permitted themselves to make offensive allusions until the second, when they saw that it continued. Mademoiselle Raymonde had ended by guessing that Evelyne was suffering from a trouble without remedy, as she suffered, herself, from the wear and tear of life. In the first week of August, at the end of a stifling day, she had joked with Mademoiselle Marthe about the stormy loves of Evelyne Gimel. The latter fingered her machine softly and did not listen. Suddenly, Mademoiselle Raymonde, who was deciphering a page of stenography, stopped, crumpled up the paper, threw it against the wall, and, mopping her forehead, eyes and throat, rested, dulled and panting, on her chair like a hunted animal. She sat for an hour without making a movement other than with her right hand, which waved her moist handker-

MADEMOISELLE GIMEL 83

chief, like a fan, before her wan and drawn face. At the moment when six o'clock struck, she said, addressing herself to Evelyne:

"I am worn out! I have no longer strength even to amuse myself, my courage is gone. And you?"

"Oh! I? When I have no more courage, I act as if I had it."

The stupid Marthe had laughed. But Raymonde, comprehending that a deep grief alone could utter words like these, had gone out with Evelyne.

"My poor friend," she had said, "I know men; they are all scoundrels alike. Yours has left you? Tell me about it, you will do me good."

Evelyne did not tell anything; but, from that day, she regained the favour of the "first stenographer" of Maclarey's bank.

At home, Evelyne and Madame Gimel met, each evening, with the same apparent joy and the same greetings as in the past. The young girl had resumed the habit of saying "mamma," and the other had never for an instant ceased to say, "my child, my daughter." They lied, both of them; they could not utter these words without thinking of the truth, which was different and cruel. Two neighbouring solitudes: that was what their home life had suddenly become. And no effort of will prevailed against the recollection, at every instant recalled. Evelyne reminded herself of the continued cares, the generosity, the tenderness, of Madame Gimel. "I love her just as much," she thought. Madame Gimel asked herself:

"Have I not always known what Evelyne has just learned? We will continue to be for each other what we have been." Together, yes, but separated; the air from without ran between them. Conversation became less spontaneous. They no longer confided everything to each other. Even the two troubles were different. Madame Gimel, who had more tenderness than imagination, thought the theatre might distract Evelyne. There was only the Théâtre Français; the Opéra Comique was closed during the dog-days. But *Britannicus* was very heavy, after a day of stenography. And then, would that audience of strangers and insignificant provincials interest Evelyne?

"How I regret *Mignon*," cried Madame Gimel, "and *Lakmé!*"

She fell back on cinematographs and the small theatres still open. They organised parties for the third gallery, or the third box at the side. To do this they had to break open a savings-bank, shaped like an apple, in which the savings destined for a trip to Dieppe reposed. Sometimes Evelyne was amused, and at other times she seemed so utterly indifferent to the piece to which she was supposed to be listening that Madame Gimel thought:

"Poor dear, she has her own play in her heart, and it is not a gay one!"

An excursion to an aunt's, living at Charenton; a dinner at the house of a friend of the late Monsieur Gimel, in the direction of Bercy; and some "surprises" in the shape of desserts when they dined at the rue Saint-Honoré; and flowers, roses, carnations, a bunch of mignonette; but nothing brought back the old smile any more, the one which said: "Life is sweet, Mamma! Watch me live!"

Madame Gimel thought of nothing else. "Such a fine offer! A handsome man and an officer! Mine was only an adjutant. It is true, he was in the Guard! All that has been lost, because a father and a mother were lacking—I mean their names. I understand Evelyne's refusal. For it was she who withdrew, she who was not willing! She is proud, but it is killing her!"

She was so filled with this idea, and so unhappy at having no one to confide in, that, without saying a word to Evelyne, she went to talk with Madame Mauléon. The former saleswoman, still "distinguished" in her appearance, and Madame Mauléon, simply affable and easy, quickly agreed and gossiped for a long time. As she went out, Madame Gimel said, with rather an affected air:

"Do it, if you dare, my dear Madame Mauléon. I should never dare."

The next day, however, she returned to the creamery of the rue Boissy d'Anglas. It was in the middle of the afternoon, the hour which belonged to the flies, to the noise of the street, and the nap of the mistress. Madame Gimel seated herself on the left of the white desk, where, so often, Evelyne had leaned; she drew a paper out of her reticule, which she unfolded and began to read, with a little affectation and much emotion, articulating better than actors at the Comédie, lowering the voice and sighing, without meaning to do so, punctuating phrases sometimes with a move of her silk-gloved hand. Madame Mauléon listened seriously, her chin resting on her hands, her vague eyes ready to fill with tears. As her new friend read, the mistress of the creamery grew excited; a smile of content, of enjoyment, of approval, distended her lips, revealing her teeth, which were fine.

There passed, after that, fifteen long days, during which Madame Gimel was strangely agitated. She had such long fits of abstraction, looking at "her daughter," that the latter asked her:

"What is the matter? What are you thinking of? I am sure that you have not heard one word of what I have said to you."

It was true, she scarcely slept, she grew thin and pale, so much so that Evelyne, one Sunday, herself broke the silence which she had imposed. Madame Gimel, returned from a rather short walk which they were accustomed to take together, between four and five, when the weather was fine—the Champs Elysées, around the Arc de Triomphe, and returning by Avenue de Friedland—stopped at the corner of the rue Faubourg Saint-Honoré and, seeing an omnibus coming down, she said:

"Let us take this to the Filles-du-Calvaire; I am tired out."

Then, between the two women, jolted upon the same bench, quite in the rear of the bus, words were exchanged which the other passengers did not hear:

"Tell me, Mamma, is it on my account that you are suffering?"

"Yes."

"You do not blame me, however, for what I did?"

"No, my poor darling! You acted like a—" she hesitated for the comparison, which made a little silence. "Like a saint!"

"You do not blame Monsieur Morand either?"

"No."

"Then, since nothing can be changed, you must cure yourself like me. You must take care of yourself, in the first place. This is the season for the seashore. I offer you, from my savings and your own, a ticket for Trouville. You will go and pass a week or two there, and you will come home cured!"

"And you?"

"I? I will keep at work, I do not need a change." To Evelyne's great surprise, Madame Gimel, a moment after, resumed, gazing through the arched window:

"My child, I am expecting a remedy, which I have asked for and which does not come."

That evening they both felt so tired that they went to bed without having dined. And they realised that silence is worth more than half confidences.

Until Monday, the 12th, no incident broke the monotony of work at the bank or of the life at home. Evelyne had breakfasted as usual at Madame Mauléon's creamery; but since the project of marriage had been abandoned, she avoided talking with the mistress of the creamery, contenting herself with a friendly nod on entering and leaving. It was exactly three forty-five when the sound of military music blew into the room where the stenographers were at work and stopped the other music short. Mademoiselle Raymonde was the first to rise; she executed a galop step, shaking out her skirt, and said:

"I am going. I never miss going to look at them!"

Mademoiselle Marthe said:

"I dislike their trade, but I am going all the same."

Evelyne hesitated a moment, and then followed her companions. The three young women ran to the end of the corridor at the left, and leaned out of the window. A regiment was passing, marching up the Boulevard Malesherbes, all the brass instruments playing. The First company, — the Second company, the men marched quickly,—the Third company, with an officer as file-closer with the nervous gait of an Alpine climber, a tall man with square chin, short moustache, and flat cheeks, a young man who kept his eyes fixed, as the regulations require, twenty paces to the front, arrived opposite Maclarey's bank, and turning his head, saw the three young women at the window, saluted with his sword, and marched on. The act was quick, but it was seen.

"Well, there, my dear! it was you that he saluted?"

"No, indeed, it was you!"

"It was you!"

MADEMOISELLE GIMEL 89

An immoderate burst of laughter from Raymonde and from Marthe. The window is closed. What matters the rest of the parade? They go back to the room of the copyists. Mademoiselle Raymonde has no trouble in guessing the emotion of Evelyne. She surprised, at the very moment when the officer saluted, an involuntary movement of recoil from her neighbour. Astonishment? Protest? Anger? In any case proof and confession.

"You are not acquainted with him, Marthe?"

"No."

"Then, it is you that he saluted, Evelyne, there is not the slightest doubt. Why do you deny it? He is very good-looking, your lieutenant."

"You must introduce him to us."

"Does he come to wait for you when you leave the bank?"

Evelyne denied shamelessly. She had wit and she became animated—the machines did not click very rapidly—and her two companions began to doubt, when, under pretext of orders to transmit, of information to give to the service of stenography, Monsieur Amédée, and another assistant secretary, and Monsieur Honoré Pope, the cashier with oily hair, one after the other, put in an appearance in the room of the stenographers. They had no doubts. Through the grating of the ground-floor window they had seen the lieutenant's salute; had heard the burst of laughter from the window above; an infallible instinct warned them that but one of the three women would have been saluted in that way by an officer! This Evelyne, who pleased every one and whom no one appeared to please. Monsieur Amédée, as usual, came sliding over the floor—he was a man of the world; he had, between his eyebrows, the crease of the man burdened with important interests; in his eyes, that little will-o'-the-wisp flame which belied the wrinkle, the gravity, and the busy look. He bent over Mademoiselle Raymonde's table, but he kept his eyes fixed on Evelyne, engaged and bending over her machine; and, on going away, provoked at not having been the object of the slightest attention:

"My compliments, Mademoiselle Evelyne; he is a fine fellow."

Evelyne blushed, turned her head; he had glided back, gained the door and disappeared.

It was the turn of the assistant secretary, who smiled with a knowing air, saying:

"Mesdemoiselles, I salute you."

Then, the second cashier, Monsieur Honoré Pope, came in, carrying a bundle of papers under his athletic arm, weakened by fat.

"Come, here is work to keep you going, my children!" said he.

Purposely he placed the bundle on Evelyne's table and took a long time to unfasten the strap, which permitted him to touch Evelyne's elbow. At the second touch, the latter got farther off without stopping her work. The big man, who only spoke with half of his mouth, the other remaining closed, said, aiming at the left and downward:

"It is not worth while to put on such airs, Mademoiselle Evelyne! You are known now!"

"Old satyr! You ought to be ashamed of yourself!"

"What did you say?"

"I said, old satyr!"

"Very well! You will hear from me, Mademoiselle Evelyne!"

"Possibly I may, but I will never ask for news of you, Monsieur Honoré Pope, and if Monsieur Maclarey questions me, I will tell him why you attack me!"

She rose. The cashier assumed an air of offended dignity; picked the bundle of papers up and carried it to Mademoiselle Raymonde, who smiled affably. But scarcely had the man disappeared than the same words, from the table in front, which was Raymonde's, and from the table in the rear, where Marthe worked, reached Evelyne's ears:

"Come! come, don't be rash! You are right, he is odious! But, all the same, it is not so easy to find work!"

Evelyne sat down to her copying again. But at a quarter before six she put on her hat:

"So much the worse if they see me; so much the worse if they dismiss me! I am going home!"

She went straight through the rue Saint-Honoré. She was furious with Honoré Pope; but most of all furious with Louis Morand. Madame Gimel provoked an outburst from her by saying:

"Mademoiselle, I have a little surprise——"

"And I, I have an incredible stupidity on the

part of Monsieur Louis Morand to tell you, unless I ought to call it a cruelty, of which I believed him incapable——"

"But what is it, Evelyne—what has happened again? At what time?"

"At three forty-five this afternoon. A way of calling attention to me which may have seemed to him a fine jest, but which has let loose the whole kennel of the bank on me, even that fat imbecile Honoré Pope, whom I told what I thought of him——"

"Oh! Evelyne!"

"Yes, just what I thought, and so plainly that, at this moment, I may perhaps be discharged from Maclarey's."

Madame Gimel was neither puzzled nor even very agitated.

"That would seem to me unfortunate. Let us see: tell me all just as it happened."

In five minutes Evelyne told the story of the afternoon. While she was talking and as she used very energetic language, the young girl watched the countenance of Madame Gimel with stupefaction. Madame Gimel's face was beaming. This sick, emaciated, anxious woman appeared to listen with pleasure, in any case with a kind of ironic placidity, to the story which Evelyne related.

"My child," she interrupted, "you can't understand. There is an explanation. I have announced a little surprise to you; that was to spare you; it is a great one."

"You have a lottery ticket which has won twenty-five francs?"

"Better than that; you will forgive me——"

"Go on just the same."

"Evelyne, I took upon myself to write to Madame Morand."

"Do you mean to the mother of Monsieur Morand, who came here? To the Madame Morand, who lives at Bugey?"

"The same. I told her that you loved her son still."

"But you know nothing about it!"

"I told her that you were a remarkable woman, a charming character, an industrious and a poor child, one who suffers too much——"

She stopped breathless, unable to utter the remaining words. Evelyne listened, pale and bewildered.

"The letter was beautiful, I assure you; Madame Mauléon told me it was. My dear child, what I dared not hope for has happened! Madame Morand has answered. I have found a true mother; I have her letter; take it, read it, my treasure! I am not able!"

She began to sob, leaning back in the low chair, happy at last to cry before a witness, which is a confession, a sharing of your trouble; happy, now that she began to hope and that she could give way to her feelings without the risk of agitating too much her adored Evelyne, her child with the nut-brown hair, reading the letter in front of her.

Evelyne was reading a letter, written in a fine slanting hand, without flourishes or erasures, upon a sheet of paper edged with black.

"Le Haut-Clos, August 10, 190—.
"Madame:
"I was deeply affected on receiving your letter. The more so as, almost by the same mail, I received one from my Louis, so unhappy, so gloomy and so resolute, alas! that I would have liked to have flown to Paris to advise him and console him, to keep him from taking a resolution, very noble of him, but which would kill me. I know him too well not to know that the distance from word to deed is short with him. He wishes to exchange with an officer of the French Congo or the Soudan. He has already made application for the exchange. I shall lose him, unless I succeed in making possible a plan which is fraught with impossibilities. As for him, he has given up seeking. But I am a mother; I still am seeking. I have thought so much about it and I will add, that you may know me better, I have prayed over it so much, that I cannot despair. I am still in darkness, but I am searching for light. I will confess to you very frankly that, without my son's knowledge, I have made inquiries about you and about Mademoiselle Evelyne. The answers have been as favourable as I could hope or fear, I hardly know which of the two words fits. I wish to see this child, whom cowardly parents have abandoned. She will know, if we must forever remain strangers to each other, that I do not think that I have the right to be hard, and that I have wished to see, to hear and to pity, at least, the one whom my son had chosen.
" Madame Théodore Morand.
"P.S. My son is ignorant of my step. He will not be at home. If Mademoiselle Evelyne can

only spend the day at Haut-Clos she may arrive very early. I rise with the dawn."

"Well! Evelyne, what shall I answer? She is a woman, this Madame Morand, she is a true mother, isn't she?"

"You did the same before her, Mamma, and you did still better! You could not know what a little wretch I might turn out and yet you took me. This lady wishes only to have an interview with me. It is kind of her all the same."

All the old intimacy, and gratitude besides, was found in these words, which Madame Gimel had bent forward to hear and to which she listened still. Madame Gimel ceased to weep.

"What do you want me to say to her?"

Evelyne reread the letter and raised her eyes to the light of the street.

"I must go," she said.

"That is what I think. When shall we go?"

The eyes, which were wandering over the roofs opposite, lengthened a little but did not wholly smile.

"Mamma, I prefer to take all the responsibility of what may happen on myself. If I make a mistake, if I do not manage well, there will be no one but myself to blame. Let me go alone. You shall be informed of the slightest details, I promise you. Next Thursday will be Assumption Day; I will ask Monsieur Maclarey for leave. If necessary, Monsieur Honoré Pope will indorse it, so that he may appear to be a generous man without rancour. We will pass the day together, Mamma, and I will leave on Thursday evening. I hope that there is an evening train for Bugey. Just where is Bugey, do you know?"

"Here is your small school atlas," said Madame Gimel, "and I have a last year's time-table, too."

They spent the evening in arranging the journey which Evelyne was to make, and in anticipating, and in fearing that it would not be a pleasure. But, nearly always, the unknown resolves itself into hope. They ended by being a little hopeful. The future, the way in which they pictured it, the words of welcome, the probable questions, the objections, all these things echoed in this room, where two poor women, one young and the other old, were talking, eager about a love which seemed to be reviving.

VI.

HAUT–CLOS.

At six o'clock on Friday morning, August 16, Evelyne descended from the P.-L.-M. train at the station of Artemare. She was alone; the morning was foggy; you could see only a small stony knoll on the left of the road, some meadows on the right, and the silhouettes of poplars in the fog. Giving her ticket to the station-master, Evelyne asked:

"Which is the road to Linot, Monsieur, if you please?"

MADEMOISELLE GIMEL 97

"Above there, Mademoiselle. You cross the village—people living in market-places have simple villages—go straight ahead, then you come to a path which mounts to Don; Linot is on the hill above Don."

He followed with his eyes, a moment, the young girl, very simply dressed, but with her hair so well arranged, such well-fitting shoes, and who walked so daintily, carrying her closed parasol on her left arm, and holding in her right hand a bag. Her sailor hat trimmed with tulle, her fair hair, her slim, straight neck, her dress, which undulated right and left to the sure rhythm of the Parisian step, were soon but a moving shadow amongst others which were motionless. The station-master went inside. Evelyne crossed the village of Artemare and took the road which rises in a steep ascent from the valley of Virieu to the lofty valley of Valromey. At first the road went along by the side of perpendicular rocks, which support the weight of the high plain and which bar, in a straight line, like the dam of a great, dried-up river, the whole space between Mount Colombier and the mountain of Colère; it turned; it passed through the village of Don, turned again, and stopped on the edge of the plateau. When Evelyne reached that point, she felt that the air was lighter, the fog was mingled with sunshine. There were several roads, and some foot-paths scaling vineyards, but no more houses. She asked the way to Linot of a middle-aged workman, on his knees before a pile of stones, who took off his glasses to see her better, and seated himself upon the heels of his wooden shoes with a slow movement.

"You have only to go straight to the station, my pretty one. You will find the road there. You will spoil your parasol and your fine little yellow shoes trying to climb the hill as we do."

A laugh, a light laugh, rippling like a line of music, rang out in the calm morning air.

"How good your country air is to breathe!" said Evelyne, flattered. "If I could breathe the like at Paris I would deny myself milk every morning."

"Then you are from Paris?"

"Where else should I be from? Is it much farther to Haut-Clos?"

"A young lady's promenade! Ah! that cursed Paris! I have a son who might have gone there, if he had wished. But here he is; he has a place at Montpellier. Cursed Paris, I say, all the same!"

He put his glasses back on his nose and began breaking stones again; the noise of the hammer and that of Evelyne's heels on the dry, convex road echoed together for a little time. Soon Evelyne moderated her Parisian gait, not that she felt at all tired, but for fear of being red on arriving. It was half past seven when she reached the top of the hill of Linot, and she recognised immediately, beyond a group of farm buildings and orchards, upon a smooth and slightly raised part of the plateau, the house where she was expected. It was the very one which she had seen in the photograph, and of which Louis Morand had spoken with so much love at Madame Mauléon's.

Only the lateral façade could be seen, irregularly pierced with a door, with one large window and three small ones. Even on this side, the slate roof, bent down on account of snow, made a blue triangle across the top of the white gable. The southern façade, toward the plain of Artemare and of Virieu, must be the principal one. It looked upon a sloping garden, surrounded by a hedge-row of trees, at whose foot there was a vineyard, doubtless the vineyard from which it received the name of Haut-Clos.

Back of it on the north side, Evelyne recognised also the walnut-tree, where an ivy-vine was climbing. It grew isolated, protecting the house, in an uncultivated piece of ground, a kind of pasture-land, to which succeeded, still veiled with the fog, strips of herbs of different heights, some green, others light, whose names Evelyne could not have told. She advanced to within fifty yards, and listened with a beating heart. Despite the letter, which said: "I rise with the dawn," how could she dare to knock or to ring at the door of that house? No sound! Seven thirty-five. At this hour her companions of the bank were scarcely awake, and Madame Gimel had not yet put the kettle on the gas-stove.

Evelyne felt her heart beat less quickly and the freshness of the air pulsate through her lungs, in the veins of her neck, and her temples. She drew three deep breaths, her lungs wide open and tasting the mountain mist, and she repeated:

"How good the air is here!"

And the third time she heard a step behind

her. A woman was coming, by a field path,
barely marked, between a patch of clover and a
bed of stubble. She was small, rather stout,
dressed in mourning, the material of which was not
new and the cut old; she had bright blue eyes
under brown lashes, and as she walked she looked
at Evelyne. She had been looking at her for
some time, no doubt, and with so intent, so steadfast a gaze that her whole face wore an expression of curiosity and intentness. She was not
preparing to smile. When she was within a few
steps of the young girl she stopped and drew a
deep breath in her turn, but with an effort and
turning very pale, like one whom emotion seizes
and stifles, she said:

"I expected to be here before you, Mademoiselle.
You must have come up rapidly. How much you
resemble the description that he gave me!"

Then only she came up close to her and reached
out her hand, but without being able to smile.
Her eyes, which were looking at Evelyne, were trying to read a whole future in her, and they were
filled with anguish. She said:

"Do I make you afraid? You are so pale."

"I think that we are both afraid, Madame.
That is not astonishing, especially in my case.
And it is true that I am afraid of you."

"A Parisienne! I thought them bolder than
we."

"Oh! being a Parisienne makes no difference,
when——"

"Say on."

"When one loves, Madame— I am not timid,

ordinarily, but to-day it is another thing. I come perhaps to learn that I shall displease you."

The old lady replied seriously:

"I shall tell you so, if it is so. Come, you must be hungry."

The two women began walking, one near the other, toward the house.

"This is my place," said Madame Morand; "it is not large——"

"The country must be pretty."

"You will be able to judge of it later; the fog will lift in half an hour. Things have not changed in my home these fifty years or more. But those who once lived here with me have left me alone! I love the place still because of them; anywhere else I should be a little more alone. My room has a small window on this side and a large one on the side of the low valleys. When it is fine weather I can watch my son coming up to Linot, almost from Virieu. He passes three weeks every year with me. That is my provision of happiness for the eleven months which follow—not all of it, however! I am never bored."

"Nor I, Madame, except when Mademoiselle Raymonde complains of fate."

"Who is she?"

"A stenographer like myself at Maclarey's."

Evelyne was taller, by half a head at least, than Madame Morand. She saw the commencement of a smile upon the wrinkled lips. She observed, without danger of being discovered, from the corner of her eye, the one who was pointing out to her the house, the garden, and the vineyard.

"You see the arbour by the side of the hedge, Mademoiselle? It is there that——"

Evelyne studied this face, a trifle too full, wrinkled in circles and reduced to a single tone, which the blood no longer vivified, but which could still turn pale; the chapped lips; the round, commonplace nose; the admirable expression of the eyes and brow; one of those transparent brows, through which one divines the upright flame of the mind; a serene look and paring of the tenderness of the soul, before which the world is like a thing already past. They walked for some hundred paces: Madame Morand entered, through the gate, into a part of the enclosure which surrounded the lateral façade of the dwelling, and from there into the kitchen, where the maid, a tall and good-natured girl from Isère, drew back before the Parisienne, bending to one side to see her dress better. Madame Morand entered first, opening and closing the doors, which had great locks.

"Come in here, Mademoiselle Evelyne," she said at last; "your coffee must be ready. Yes, it is. Eat first, and then we will talk. The sun is going to make us a visit, you see the whole garden is bright."

In fact the garden was bright; it reached to the door of the sitting-room—a large room, hung with faded paper and furnished with mahogany covered with flowered cretonne; it entered even a little on each side of the French window which was wide open; the borders, in gratitude, sent up on the parquet some adventurous branches, such as there are in all clusters. Out of the corner

MADEMOISELLE GIMEL 103

on the right, a bunch of mignonette, on the left a stalk of marshmallow. In front, the central path led down, edged with rose-trees, of which not one was rare, but which were as prolific as common, happy people.

Evelyne seated herself before the low table on which Madame Morand was accustomed to keep her work-basket, and on which this morning were placed, upon a spotless napkin, the coffee-pot, cup, sugar-bowl, some butter, some jam, and the cream-jug. She began to bite a slice of bread and jam, which gave her courage to smile for the first time.

"What are you smiling at?" asked the old lady, who often went as far as the village to see a child smile.

"I was smiling at a saying one often hears in the creameries: 'There is fresh butter only in Paris.' Mamma says the same; Madame Gimel, I mean—that is—you know, the one who brought me up."

The smile faded away; Evelyne became red. Tears rose to the corners of her eyes. She pretended to be interested in the arbour of boxwood in the rear of the garden. Madame Morand, who could have spoken, and dissipated the memory, and consoled her, did nothing; but she looked in silence into the eyes of flax-grey which the light illumined to their very depths, down to the sorrowful soul which was struggling to recover itself.

That same day, at two o'clock in the afternoon, the postman who passed by Haut-Clos carried a letter from Evelyne, who wrote to Madame Gimel:

"You must know all; I promised you, I keep my word. Then, at eight o'clock, after the reception of which I have just told you, I had cried stupidly, for nothing, when Madame Morand, who until then had been standing, came and seated herself against the light, turning her back to the garden. And this little person began an examination! . . . How many things she asked me! She questioned me about you, about my education, about what I thought of plays which I have seen, my work at the bank, everything, finally, with more details than her son had done, oh! much more! He believed in me more quickly. With her I was conscious only that her distrust was lessening. I was a person from a long way off, from the dangerous city, from the place where men ruin themselves for women who are daring. I kept my self-possession, I told her:

"'Madame, it is just the contrary; men are the ones who ruin women. I know something about it?'

"'Really?'

"'Like all those who are virtuous. Men have such audacity! With poor girls like us, they don't stand on ceremony, I assure you, in the street, in the omnibus, in stairways, at the restaurant!'

"'The blackguards!'

"'Often well-dressed men, with monocles. Young and old, they stare at you, they say anything to you.'

"'Why, I should blush! What do you answer?'

"'Nothing, unless they are a little too bold. You simply walk on; pretend not to hear; sometimes you go into a shop. Oh! there is an apprenticeship to serve. I have served mine. I could pass between two files of gendarmes.'

"'You are brave, my child!'

"'I am not all that I should be, Madame, but brave, yes a little. And I am not the only one. The brave ones are more numerous than you would believe; and if you wish me to tell you a thought which I have often: virtue, at Paris, is altogether *chic;* it is vaccinated, tried, stamped, and, with it all, it is good-humoured. I have some friends who have no imposing airs; but when you know them well, you discover virtue in them, and real virtue. The majority would make charming wives. There are many proud ones among them, some sensitive ones, princesses of elegance, some clever ones.' I stopped, comprehending that I had gone too far. Madame Morand did not reply directly. She said:

"'You blush, Mademoiselle Evelyne? You are very wrong. I believe what you say. Come, let me help you to some preserves. They are preserves of mountain raspberries, such as you have never tasted at Paris.'

"For the first time I felt that I was not displeasing. The thought made me so happy that I obeyed Madame Morand and realised that I was hungry.

"The inspection of the house—which is not

beautiful, which looks like the pilot-house that we saw together, you remember, at Dieppe the day of the excursion—took three good quarters of an hour. It was ten o'clock when we went out of doors. Ah! how delightful if he had been there to show me his own country. Sunshine everywhere; the fog flown away; more land under my eyes than I had ever seen in my life, stretched out before us, in the hollow where I had climbed this morning up to Linot. I cannot say how many low valleys, villages, dear little hills and mountains. It is dreamland. Around us, to the right, to the left, more mountains, but close by and dotted with forests, and, between the wide slopes, little hills covered with vineyards, meadows, houses.

"'We are in the high valley, you see,' Madame Morand said, 'and upon the hill of Linot; a little farther, there is the hill of Hostel, with its vineyards and lime-trees; then that of Arcollière——'

"She took pleasure in saying these familiar names. But I kept thinking that she did not talk to me of her son. We walked in the footpaths of the peasants, often on the grass, and she stopped to ask me:

"'You are not tired?'

"I answered:

"'Madame, I am much more tired when I have worked seven hours at stenography and typewriting. Then it is my shoulders that are stiff with fatigue, and my fingers that have lost their energy. On the mountain, to-day, I could walk until night.'

"We came to a road; she placed herself by my

MADEMOISELLE GIMEL 107

side and said to me with a tone which was, I think, a reward and which I had earned:

"'This morning when I met you, Mademoiselle Evelyne, I was returning from mass. I go every day. My whole strength comes from that. Now that I know you, and that I see that you are a child naturally noble, and so sincere, I can confess to you the dearest wish I have made for my Louis——'

"We stood facing each other on the road between two great hedges of brambles. She became pale again as at the first moment when she had seen me. But she was looking at me with eyes in which there was love for me, and which recalled yours to me. She continued:

"'Mademoiselle Evelyne, I have wished all my life that my son should marry a religious woman. Those who are fairly good without religion, with prayer would be still more worthy of admiration. It is a world closed to many. I do not wish to preach a sermon to you, I ask you to tell me sincerely if your dear young soul could rise to that height?'

"I have never looked in eyes as beautiful as hers, which were waiting and which were repeating:

"'Your dear young soul, could it rise?'

"I answered:

"'Why not? I have thought more than once on what you say to me. It has not come into my life, that is all.'

"'If you should seek?'

"'You believe that it would be a way of loving him better?'

"'I am very sure of it, my child.'

"I shut my eyes. I stretched out my hands a little, and I felt this old mother, very tender as you are, weeping on my breast. And I leaned my head down against hers; when I was able to speak, I said to her, resuming my walk by her side:

"'Madame, I wish to tell you everything, in my turn.... I am sure that no one will love your son as I love him; but I should be an obstacle to his career; even were I religiously such as you would wish me to be, I should still have my wretched civil status of foundling. There are doors which would close before us, or which would open only half-way to the superior officer, by order. I am very unhappy, I assure you! I ought not to have come; if we should talk it over together, he and I, we would come to the same conclusion: I cannot marry him! Indeed, no! I ought not to have come. I had already made the sacrifice once, and it will be harder to make it again.... Have you a solution? Have you a way?'

"Like myself she was in tears. Walking along she put her poor mourning bonnet straight, which I had displaced with my arms. And she was silent.

"Soon we saw the houses of the hamlet of Vieu; the paths, the scenery between the trees and above the meadows in relief, were perhaps pretty: I did not see them. We went in the church; Madame Morand made me go in first, and I stepped at once to the holy water basin, then, naturally, I turned to her to offer the holy water, which astonished her. We were alone. She went a little way up the nave and knelt down. I re-

MADEMOISELLE GIMEL

mained in the last row of chairs. And it is certain that I felt better than usual; I said a true prayer and I did not notice the time my prayer lasted.

"Madame Morand touched my shoulder; we went out; she said to me simply:

"'I have a commission to give to Angélique Samonoz. We will go this way, if you please.'

"At the grocer's, I saw from the threshold, where I very sadly waited for her, that she was discussing terms, that she counted out some money, that she wrote something. But what did it matter to me? I was only struck with the joyousness of her face when we regained the road to Haut-Clos. She turned her head toward me, she sought for something besides the commonplace smile, the ordinary smile which I gave her. What did she wish? Could I guess? At the last house of the village, without warning me, she took my hand and pressing it:

"'Little Mademoiselle Evelyne, be happy!'

"'Why, Madame?'

"'I have just sent a messenger to the post-office of Champagne. I have telegraphed to my son.'

"'What did you say to him?'

"'To come.'

"'When will he be here?'

"'To-morrow morning, and I shall keep you.'

"Mamma, I will not tell you of the return to the house of Haut-Clos. We talked only of Louis. I am filled with a joy that cannot be described. It is only trouble that one tells at length. I have but one now, which struggles in the midst of my happiness, like a fly in cream, and which I cannot make fly away, and it is this: What career to find for Louis if he gives up the army? Is it not too much to ask of a man?

"Until to-morrow,
"EVELYNE.

"P.S. Do not look for my photograph. I brought it with me. Was it a presentment? I would be so happy not to bring it back."

The next day, at the same hour, Evelyne wrote a second letter:

"HAUT-CLOS, Saturday.

"He arrived this morning, not by the road as I did, no, by footpaths known only to the inhabitants of the country, and rough ones, I assure you. He took half an hour less than I to climb from Artemare to Haut-Clos. He is an energetic man, and it was not only seeing him run across the fields and jump over palings which has best proved this energy to me. Madame Morand waited for her son at the same place. Although she had gone to bed very late—ten o'clock, Mamma, a dissipation at Linot, a date in the mountains!—she had risen with the dawn, visited the kitchen, the linen-room, then the garden. She was like a partridge in a cage. All along the hedge, on the edge of the vineyard, she trotted without a hat, her head covered with a shawl. At times, she lifted herself up on the tip of her sabots, watching with eyes and ears for her Lieutenant, my Lieutenant. I was in the sitting-room, behind the window. We distributed our rôles yesterday evening. She wished to speak with him first, to tell him all alone what we had both of us said, to act the mother finally a last time. I saw him bending between two lines of vines, straightening up, raising his hand. A shadow leaps over the fence. It is he; I see him kissing his mother, questioning her, taking her arm, trying to pull her along. She resists laughingly. Ah! he loves me still. He looks very well in a short jacket and cap, his legs gaitered like an Alpine climber. He seemed to me taller than at Paris. He comes, positively, by the central path, between the old rose-trees, on the arm of Madame Morand. He keeps his eyes fastened on the window, where I no longer am. I have run to the door and I have opened it.... Then, Mamma, we stood looking at each other, I on the threshold, they in the path, motionless, struck with joy. I thought that I was going to faint; I made a great effort; I said:

"'Monsieur, I love you always, but you must not sacrifice your career for me, you must not regret' . . .

"He dropped Madame Morand's arm, he came up to me, and, with my permission, he kissed me and with his whole heart, I assure you. Then he said:

"'You are my betrothed, now; come, let us talk of the future.'

"We passed a part of the morning in the house, all three of us, and the rest, we two, in the country around Haut-Clos. Louis wished to show me the nooks of the country where are lodged still, as he says, all the memories of his youth. We were, and we are, very happy. We talked about so many things that were I merely to try to enumerate them, it would be a real task, a very pleasant one, but too long for a letter to tell you. The sky was clear, all the cultivated strips of land flowed around us on the slopes and moved in the wind like a wave of new ribbons. Louis asked me:

"'Do you like the country?'

"'I do not know it.'

"'I adore it. If I come back here, will you love it?'

"'I love you, and everywhere it will be the same.'

"Madame Morand, to whom we told this conversation, took on an expression, a little sad, and she declared:

"'How long have people been saying these sweet words, and how they keep the world alive!'

"Oh! yes, to live! I feel that I am living and I, who used not to cling to the hours, cling to the minutes now. In my turn, I asked:

"'Do you remember the 12th of August? Maclarey's bank, the regiment which marched by, your salute with your sword? I was angry with you for it. Why did you salute me?'

"'Because, the evening before I had received word that I would not get the exchange to Soudan. My resolution had been taken a week before to resign if I did not obtain Soudan and, since my career was the obstacle between us, to suppress the obstacle. . . . That is what I am going to do. . . . In saluting you I was in my right, you see.' . . . He added:

"'I have but one vocation; but for you, Evelyne, I can have a trade.'

"How sweet these words are, are they not? You understand that I am flattered, touched, and that I, the laughing one, have wept listening to them. He is simple, he is good, he has a quick power of decision which gives one confidence. I said to him besides:

"'Do you know what pleased me, at once, in you?'

"'What? My uniform?'

"'No, it is not as pretty as a dress.'

"'My mustache?'

"'Too short.'

"'Then I will let it grow. My soldierly air?'

"'The affectionate one suits me better.'

"'I can guess no more. Tell me yourself.'

"'What enraptured me was that you showed respect for me; we are not accustomed to it. . . .'

"That is how things are. A single thing troubles us.

"How and by what career to replace the army, where Louis cannot remain? He is young, he is going to try at Paris, at first, for love of me. I close this long letter quickly. Perhaps it will reach you at the same time that I do. . . . I leave this evening. They will take me to the station in a carriage. Louis will not leave the mountains for two days. Good-bye.

"EVELYNE."

VII.

THE DOUBLE VISIT.

As soon as he returned to Paris, Louis Morand donned his uniform and repaired to the house of his colonel, who lived, Place de Jéna, above the gardens and the Seine. It was ten o'clock in the morning. The lieutenant's leave did not expire until the next day, which was what Colonel Ridault observed to begin with, on seeing the officer come to him:

"You have changed your habits of old," he said. "Four days' leave, four days passed in the Ain. You would return to Paris at five o'clock in the morning, and, at six, you were at Pépinière. Can you be growing old?"

"It may be, Colonel."

"Well, I am not. Look at this. Is not the plan of my fortress rather attractive? Imagine the sea on this side, and there, the background of the bay of Villefranche; the terraces, you remember, baked and golden, like loaves of bread?"

"I have never been able to travel, Colonel; I do not know the place, but the house will be pleasant, certainly."

It was a wonderfully beautiful day. Sunshine and air stirred by the current of the river entered the study, which, without the rack of pipes hanging on the side of the chimney, would have been all in the style of Louis XV. The colonel, in a light jacket, seated before his desk, was studying an architect's sketch, a brilliant water-colour, which represented a low villa, roofed with tiles, whose windows seemed cut in the clumps of bougainvilléas. He raised his head, shoved his armchair back a little, trying to read in the countenance of the lieutenant the progress or the cure of a trouble of love, of which he had been the first confidant.

"Your face is always a sealed book, my dear Morand. I read there, however, that your mind is more fixed. Come, come! Here, you are turning pale! What is the matter? A tear! I do not recognise you! Is this indeed one of my officers?"

"Who is going to leave the regiment."

"You mean to exchange?"

"I resign."

"You? But I forbid you!"

"Colonel!"

"I do not want you even to speak of it to me! My duty is to prevent suicides, Morand; to watch over the honour of the regiment. Very well! By giving in your resignation, you will commit suicide, for you are the most military of all my officers: a man of discipline, who takes duty like bread, every day, and who finds it good; the man to whom I would confide a battalion in a war, and whom all the soldiers would follow, sounding the charge. But don't you know what it is that makes the chief? It is not gold lace, it is the heart which never trembles, the clear eye, the sharp command, it is the continual thought for others and the forgetfulness of self, and that, all that, Morand, you have."

The colonel had suddenly come near the young

man and had seized him by the shoulder, which he pressed in his strong hand, as if to show that Morand was his prisoner, and that the regiment would not let him go. At the same time the duel of glances went on, touching and swift, between these two men, separated only by an arm's length. The old soldier ordered, begged, was astonished not to conquer and became again the offended superior officer whose blue eyes, charged with will, commanded imperiously; while before him, wide open in the full light, the brown eyes of the lieutenant, a moment troubled and moist, refused to say yes and grew more and more gloomy.

"I would never have believed that of you, Morand!" cried the colonel, letting him go.

Choking with rage, he buttoned his linen jacket, threw himself down in the armchair and began hitting, with his paper-knife, the water-colour of the fortress spread out before him. Morand straightened a little more; his eyes had not swerved, they had not yielded:

"Colonel, I have resolved to marry the young girl of whom I spoke to you. I sacrifice to her my vocation as a soldier, and all the labour that I have had to win my rank."

"It is madness! It is sheer madness!"

"That is possible, Colonel, but it will happen, this very evening."

"No, Monsieur!"

"I shall write my letter to the minister. It was my duty to notify you; it is done."

"No, it is not done! Morand, do not leave us.

MADEMOISELLE GIMEL 117

For the love of the army, which has but too many cowards. No, I mean——"

The lieutenant saluted and turned to the door.

"Morand, my boy, I cannot let you go thus. Come back! I have something more to ask you."

Colonel Ridault had risen, and he brought the lieutenant back to the open window. He had spoken these last words with such an accent of affection and sorrow that, suddenly, all the artificial harshness and even the natural firmness of Morand gave way.

"You may believe, Colonel, that the battle has been fierce for me; I would rather have fought that battle for which I have been trained, the true one, that of arms——"

"Not so! The true battle is that of every day; and those who do not betray their honour in that one, do not forfeit it under arms either—I do not mean to say that you are acting contrary to honour, my dear friend, no, but contrary to your own interest, contrary to your vocation, contrary to all, as you acknowledge. Tell me; is she then so charming?"

His face had a youthful smile, very brief, the first. The two men were leaning their elbows on the window-sill; before them was Paris all transparent in the summer light like a glass.

"Yes, Colonel, yes. Ah, yes!"

"The expression is too weak, is it not? The word is not strong enough?"

And the first laugh broke, discreetly, above the trees.

"Have you by chance a photograph of her, Morand?"

"For three days, Colonel. It does not leave me."

He searched in the pocket of his uniform and handed over the photograph; Colonel Ridault seized it quickly, held it to the light, then put it away as far as he could from his face, for he had become far-sighted. With the other hand he twisted the point of his mustache.

"You are right, charming is not strong enough. There is character in these eyes. Are they blue?"

"No, Colonel, clear grey."

"A rare shade. They must have a piquant and tender smile, have they not?"

"Ah, Colonel!"

"And this line of the chin, firm, a trifle plain-spoken, is not commonplace at all. And these lips, which would quickly utter a little nonsense, but never a spiteful word, and which I should believe to be supreme in pity. One is tempted to ask where race will lodge itself next? Well, then, my dear fellow, since you are sure that she is an honest girl, and as I think her as pretty as you think her yourself, will you tell me why she should not be able to modestly fill her little niche in the chorus of the 'ladies' of the regiment?"

"You know the reason——"

"Eh? Yes, her father—a Jean Jacques, of whom there remains only that. Her father might have been well born enough; he must have been even very well born. Lieutenant Louis Morand, look at me."

"I am looking."

"If I should assure you that this young woman will be received in the military world, well received even, would you renounce giving in your resignation?"

"Colonel, I thank you for your sympathy; I am deeply touched; but my resolution is taken to leave the army."

"Yes, because you think that I have changed my opinion and that the world will not change theirs. But if you had proofs to the contrary?"

"What proofs?"

"If perfectly certain proofs were given you that the most elegant, the most worldly women of the regiment will receive the visit of Madame Louis Morand, and will return this visit—for the welcome of the others, those whom I call women of heart, is not doubtful—would you still send your letter?"

"No, I should remain. But that is improbable, one may even say impossible."

"Wait three days. You promise me?"

The lieutenant, flattered and touched by the insistence of his chief, looked at Paris, where the arbiters of his fate, wholly unconscious of their rôle—wives of lieutenants, captains and majors—were, at this moment, engaged in their morning's shopping.

"So be it," he said. "I shall have obeyed to the last, Colonel. I will wait three days."

He pressed the hand which Colonel Ridault extended to him, and withdrew. The colonel made him a gesture of friendship again upon the landing-place; then, watching his young soldierly silhouette disappear on the stairway, between the walls of purple stucco, he murmured:

"Go, my boy! I wish you to be my farewell gift, my souvenir to the regiment. I will give you back to it. He does not suspect, the poor boy, that I am going to commit an act of folly for him. It is not the first in my life, but it is the best, the one which will gain for me, I hope, the pardon for several others. Bah! I have no longer anything to expect from the War Office! What do I risk? Besides, I shall affirm nothing; that would be to lie. I will let the legend shape itself and take wings. We shall see, indeed!"

He re-entered his study, whistling a march, rolled up the rather badly treated plan of his fortress, and pressed an electric button. An orderly opened the door.

"Lancret, I shall go out at two o'clock. You will get out uniform No. I."

Colonel Ridault made several visits in the course of the afternoon. He had the luck that he was hoping for, and was received by three or four of the ladies of the regiment, not the youngest ones, but those best qualified, by the number of their interests and their curiosity, to fashion a legend with a word, to put it in circulation, and to give it the authority of a bit of history. At the house of one he spoke only of the character and the eyes of Mademoiselle Evelyne; at another's, he declared that he wished to be one of the witnesses of the lieutenant, who was on the eve of making an unexpected and delicious marriage; at the third's, who asked: "But, finally, whom does she look like?" he answered:

"Like me, Madame."

That was enough. From the very next day it was whispered in the military world, that the colonel proposed to recognise the foundling later; that, meanwhile, he avowed his paternity with much frankness, with a tenderness which could not deceive anyone, and that to repair his fault he meant to give Mademoiselle Evelyne a dot. They even fixed the figure of the dot. It was modest at the beginning of the day. Toward the close some people asked:

"Do you believe that he can be so rich?"

The second day after that, several comrades congratulated the lieutenant, during the morning drill, in the court of the barracks. Every one said:

"They say that she is charming."

And when he went home, in the afternoon, the porter handed him two notes, the first of a series which was long! One read:

"Most sympathetic congratulations from our household."

The other, more explicit, said:

"MY DEAR MORAND:

"We have just learned the happy news. My wife will be charmed to make the acquaintance of Madame Louis Morand, of whom, for the last two days, every one is saying the kindest things. She wishes to present her to our best friends.

" Congratulations."

Finally, in the evening, a captain of the regiment, who returned from the War Office, affirmed that suddenly the prejudices, which had delayed the advancement of Colonel Ridault, had disappeared; and that Colonel Ridault at the next promotion would be made a brigadier-general. But the report might not have been true, and the lieutenant, that very evening, entirely forgot to mention it to Evelyne, whom he went to see again.

THE DIPLOMAT

THE DIPLOMAT.

I.

Monsieur Louis Jean Népomucene de Rabelcourt, seated under a green arbour of jasmine in the rear of his English garden, murmured:

"I am a coward!"

And, almost immediately, he added this explanation, which did not go beyond the green walls, motionless in the June heat:

"She has no one but me. I am her sole support. She called me three weeks ago, and I have not budged. I am a coward!"

Several times every day, Monsieur de Rabelcourt addressed this offensive epithet to himself without its deciding him to leave his domain of Wimmerelles, where he lived in summer, to go a quarter of an hour beyond the Belgian frontier. Short and alert, a trifle large in the waist, and with sinewy limbs; full-faced, with a ruddy complexion, and smooth-shaven, save two small side-whiskers at the base of the ear white and light as if made of silk, Monsieur de Rabelcourt belonged to that category of old men who retain their youth. Their youth consists nearly always in a peculiar quality of their mind, which their life has not disillusioned. They guard illusion, either of themselves, of science, of their profession, of the continuance or merely the curiosity of the present hour, and the enjoyment of the news of the day. Merely to look at the eyes of Monsieur de Rabelcourt, bluish-grey eyes, always quivering and vibrating, amusing themselves in looking, searching, questioning, reading another's glance or smile, you guessed that this man had a singular talent for psychology, or believed that he had. For him every visit, every meeting, even commonplace ones, assumed the appearance of a conference, and turned to experience. He appeared to ask those whom he accosted for the first time, women especially, whom he found infinitely more interesting than men: "What kind of a heart is this? Does it beat? Doesn't it beat? Will it beat? Has it a secret? Can one learn it?" And of those whom he met again after a brief interval: "Have we gone far, since the other day?"

In the gay world of Brussels, which he frequented in summer; at Paris, where he passed the winter; he had the reputation of being an agreeable conversationalist, well versed in affairs of the heart, a little too prone to enrich his observations, and of a discretion above the average, which is not to say trustworthy. He was courted, and people feared him. They enjoyed, especially in their freshness, the stories which he told; they feared those which he might surprise or invent.

All was explained, when you knew that Monsieur de Rabelcourt had been in the diplomatic

THE DIPLOMAT 127

service; and that perpetual tension of his curiosity with regard to the feminine unknown, the persistency and fluttering of his eyes, the insidious turn of his conversation, lost their singularity and became a pardonable and troublesome transposition of professional habit. They told each other that he had a diplomatic temperament, that he continued his career, interrupted by his retirement, in drawing-rooms; and if they still feared his manner, it no longer astonished them.

In two capitals at least, he passed, therefore, as a clever man. It would have been slandering him, besides, to refuse him a certain sensibility. He was fond of his memories of Washington, where he had made his début as attaché of the embassy; of Montevideo, Valparaiso and Lima, where he had slowly been promoted in rank; of Buenos Ayres, where, being made minister in that same America from which they did not transfer him, he had grown old, envious, and forgotten, he thought; he liked the despatches, which he had sent to twenty successive ministers, and which he alone knew; he loved the familiar images, which the mere word America evoked before him, of creoles, half-breeds, Spanish women and Portuguese, women who smoked and swung in hammocks, with one arm dangling, under the shade of bananas and mimosas. He liked to recall his former trips through the passes of the Cordilleras, and his present repose in the flat country on the Belgian frontier; his brick châlet, his garden, so different from the virgin forest; his Angora, which resembled a yellow caterpillar; his numerous decorations, kept in a case large as a valise; he liked his club at Brussels, where he regularly passed the week-end; he was also fond of Countess Guillaumette, his little niece, his last relative, married with a cavalry officer; the one precisely about whom Monsieur de Rabelcourt had been accusing himself, for the last three weeks, of selfishness and irresolution.

"Dear child!" he murmured under the jasmine arbour. "Barely eight years married and already unhappy! She, so pretty, so clever, so full of imagination; a little the image of my brother, a little mine, with a charm all her own! Yet I have not answered her letter! I have not flown to her! Rabelcourt, you are growing old, you dread a trip to Berry! You enjoy your repose, while Guillaumette weeps and expects you."

The old diplomat interrupted his monologue to chase, with a net, a slim white petal, curved like the snowy neck of a tiny swan, which had just settled whirling on his jacket sleeve. Then he lifted his eyes, and contemplated fondly through the arch of the arbour, with the uneasy tenderness which precedes a farewell, the elongated rectangle which formed his garden; the tall trees, crowded in a small clump on both sides, and which rose, like a green cliff, in the smooth-cut plain; the two avenues which passed under their shade encircling an oval grass plot; the turf, fresh as in April, watered every morning, clipped once a fortnight, where daisies could flourish only on condition of crouching on the ground; finally, quite at the end, through the transparent veil of shimmering air, the low red house, whose tiles were grazed here and there by branches of elm-trees, silent fans which the summer breeze set in motion.

"This is what keeps me, then?" thought Monsieur de Rabelcourt. He raised his head, which he held bent a little to see better under the wanton stems which hung from the arch and lessened the opening of the door, and he called:

"Eugène?"

At first there was no answer, then the sand of a path crackled more and more clearly under approaching steps. The valet of Monsieur de Rabelcourt, blond and formal, dressed in black, appeared at the corner of a clump of trees.

"Eugène, go to my room and pack my bag. I will take the evening express. Put in suit number two; it is for the country."

The sound of footsteps died away and was lost in the silence of the plain stifling under the sun, while Monsieur de Rabelcourt drew from his pocket a violet envelope, already worn at the corners, opened it for the twentieth time, and reread, skipping useless phrases and scanning others, a letter which he could have recited by heart.

"My Dear Uncle: First I must give you news of the children. . . . Jean, Pierre. . . . Ta, ta, ta, Louise is suffering with her teeth. . . . Ta, ta, ta. . . . Roberte. . . . Ta, ta, ta. . . . As for myself, I prefer not to reply to your affectionate questions. One should question only those who are young, gay, happy, for otherwise, you risk burdening yourself, alas, uselessly, with the troubles of others. No, dear uncle, I am no longer the smiling niece whom you remember; I would like to be able to go far away, to Buenos Ayres, to Lima and live free with you. I have had enough of life. It is too hard! Ah! one thing is certain, when my daughters are of the age to marry, I will bid them reflect twice, a hundred times. . . . But what am I saying? It is weak to complain. Forget what I have just written . . . above all do not refer to this subject; that would be disastrous. Write me rather the sequel of that story, which you began in your last letter, the story of that Madame de ——. Ta, ta, ta.

"P.S. Édouard came back from Algeria nine weeks ago. He is very well."

Monsieur de Rabelcourt drew a deep sigh, in returning the letter to his pocket, but his face, like his voice, had become more and more firm as he read:

"It is perfectly clear," he said aloud, "transparent enough! There is no need to be a diplomat to decipher that pitiful enigma! It is the eternal despatch of the yellow book of life. Guillaumette complains of her husband; she is suffering on his account; the dryness of her postscript is sufficiently eloquent: 'Édouard is very well.' He has deceived her. Where? With whom? Can it be at Limoges, where they are in garrison? I do not think so, since Monsieur de Rueil has just passed six months in Algeria, on a topographic mission, and Guillaumette's letter reveals a sorrow which breaks forth, a surprise; it is a cry! Then, what is it? I see but two suppositions: an Algerian adventure that this poor child has discovered, or an intimacy in Berry on his return, in that peaceful corner where she was so happy to pass their three months' leave. . . . I will find out what it is. She will tell me, since she has begun the confession. She calls me, since she has taken me for a confidant. I start, Guillaumette, I start, I am coming to aid you!"

He crossed the whole length of the garden, opened the box of orders, out of which he chose a decoration that Dom Pedro himself had placed on the breast of the "dear minister," and he could not refrain from smiling sadly, while passing the ribbon through his buttonhole. "I am returning to the active diplomatic list," he thought, "and it is a good omen to carry with me the evidence of my best success. May I succeed in this as I did in the affair of the Jacobson concession!"

He dined and, at nightfall, took the express from Brussels.

II.

The traveller only passed through Paris. Five or six errands between his arrival at daybreak at the North station and his departure in the afternoon from the Orleans station restored his natural vivacity, which a night of disturbances and sudden awakenings had depressed a little. When he was again settled in the train and felt that he was rolling toward the fields of Berry, from which only a few hours' journey separated him, he regained all his confidence in his diplomatic star, all the vibrating good humour, the abundance of ideas and the oratorical form, that he had formerly known the night before princely audiences, or interviews with the ministers of South America. His imagination flew before him, picturing to him the château of Monant, the old family dwelling, from which he had escaped early to roam the world. The last time that he had gone to Berry was to be present at the marriage of Guillaumette. They had postponed the wedding a month to give her uncle, the diplomat, time to reach there. How clearly he saw the two slanting towers joined by a main building, resting on a hill and surrounded with sloping chestnut groves; the tent decorated with flags and bouquets of daisies and corn-flowers for the wedding breakfast on the return from the church, and the hurried, snatched departure of the young couple, full of agitation and full of joy, who rose from the table before their guests, leaving to go to the neighbouring station, alone, but followed by the thought of all. How pretty this radiant and agitated Guillaumette was, to whom a hundred friends, Parisians, Berrichons, and Poitevins, were calling, in murmurs mingled with tears and laughter: "Good-bye, darling, adieu, Madame! Be happy. Do not forget us, Guillaumette! Think of us, dearest!" Glances were fixed on this smiling apparition, arrested a last moment between the portières, which she was holding with one hand; this face, in which each sought, with secret jealousy, with repressed sobs, with infinite desire, to read the fleeting radiance of perfect faith in life, whilst she, already separated from the others, was looking at but one person, her oldest, most faithful friend. Yes, Monsieur de Rabelcourt had had Guillaumette's last thought at the moment when childhood ended. He, protected against emotion by the long habit of separations, had wept; he, the sceptic, had believed and believed firmly in the happiness which he wished his niece and which he almost envied. This Édouard de Rueil, who was carrying Guillaumette off, taking her away from the château de Monant, was so obviously in love! Young, also, full of promise, like all officers who marry, he passed indeed as being a trifle blunt, rough and stubborn, but his comrades judged him to be of a loyal, upright nature, incapable of betrayal.

"Who would have said then?" Monsieur de Rabelcourt repeated to himself, looking at the twilight descend upon the misty plains of Berry, "who would have guessed? This Rueil, with his large neck, his arched nose, his piercing black eyes, looks like an eagle, a hawk, but not the least in the world like a fickle turtle-dove. He did not have an even temper. That must have grown upon him. In truth, I have a pretty piece of business there on my hands!"

He was a trifle disturbed by his rôle. But a little fever of self-love and anger urged him on. It was eight o'clock in the evening when he set foot on the platform of a little rural station in the midst of an almost deserted country covered with trees and fresh as a mushroom cellar.

"Oh!" he exclaimed, "what a journey! From yesterday evening at eleven! At last, here I am! I recognise the sharp air of Monant. Burning days and icy nights!" He threw his Scotch plaid over his shoulders, although he had worn his summer overcoat, and looked around him. As he had neglected to announce his coming, so as to fall "in the middle of the game," according to his favourite expression, he saw only the departing train, the station-master going inside with his lantern, and the stars which were coming out. It happened luckily that a little shepherd boy was passing, whistling, on his way to a small farm.

"Take my bag and accompany me to the château," said Monsieur de Rabelcourt. "I will reward you."

"Are you going to the ball?" asked the boy.

"To the ball? No, my boy, I am going to the château of Monant, nowhere else. There are two or three rather silly country houses about here, I know, but I am going to Monant, you understand, Monant!"

The boy looked at him, gave a toss of his head, which signified: "I made a mistake," and doubtless taking him for some business man, he led the way without uttering another word.

It was a calm night, perfumed with the odour of leaves, of wheat in grain and of gorse in bloom. Monsieur de Rabelcourt, following his guide, took the shortest way along solitary roads, walking upon the ridges of old ruts and upon slopes of grass that no scythe had ever mown. He stalked along, his head up, his nostrils to the wind, breathing in the air with full lungs. From time to time he pronounced in an undertone phrases which seemed opportune and pertinent to him:

"This is an intoxicating country, Monsieur, heady and poetic, I acknowledge that. But when a man has wife and children, devil take it! he must stay at home! After all, there is such a thing as morality."

The boy thought that he was reciting a fable. Together they went down into the hollows of the valleys; they climbed slopes where ferns shone beneath the branches of chestnut-trees. At last, after half an hour, reaching the turn of a clump of trees, which opened suddenly upon a rising glade, they found themselves at once on a gravelled walk, a hundred steps from the château, which stood on the crest of the hill, whose windows, from top to bottom, were lighted up.

"*Sapristi!*" exclaimed Monsieur de Rabelcourt, "they were not expecting me nevertheless?"

"It is because they are dancing!" said the little urchin. "They often dance. They do not put themselves out much for it."

The traveller listened a moment to the shrill notes of a piano melting into the night, and he doubted no longer. Annoyed, he continued to advance slowly, to gain his breath. Some men servants, grouped around the stables to the right of the château, were talking. One of them stepped forward, a formal old steward with thick white side-whiskers, who had served the masters of Monant for thirty years, and who had known Monsieur de Rabelcourt at the time of his diplomatic activity, at the most brilliant period of his career.

"Is it possible!" he exclaimed. "It is Monsieur le Ministre!"

"In person, Claude," replied Monsieur de Rabelcourt, flattered by a title which was not given him as frequently as of yore. "A surprise! I arrive without notice."

"Does Monsieur le Ministre desire madame to be informed?"

"Not at all! On the contrary. You may take up my bag only so that I may change my clothes, and make ready a guest-chamber for me. But what is going on this evening at Monant? A ball?"

"Pardon, Monsieur le Ministre. The rooms would not lend themselves to what is called a great ball. We have a few people of the neighbourhood, about thirty. It is only a hop. It will end at eleven o'clock, I take the liberty of assuring Monsieur le Ministre of that, because madame has already given several reunions of this kind to enliven the last weeks of monsieur's leave."

He bowed, taking the valise; and one would have said, from the air with which he passed before his comrades, that he carried the bag in which the former minister kept his despatches.

"Courageous and imprudent child," thought Monsieur de Rabelcourt, "I recognise her well! She dances to throw the world off the scent; she wants to make believe in a happiness which no longer exists. I am afraid of but one thing; that is, that the masks will drop of themselves, and too suddenly, when I enter. For I am coming, Monsieur de Rueil, and I shall be at the fête."

By the time he had changed his dress, the hall clock was just striking nine; the diplomat had crushed in his buttonhole the Brazilian ribbon, drawing the ends very tight so that they followed the line on his shirt-front of the four buttons of his white waistcoat, and, noiselessly, he pushed open the drawing-room door.

He stopped near the door. They were waltzing. No one noticed him at first, then a young woman, seated near a dowager, and who was looking around for a topic of conversation, seeing the unknown, bent forward and asked:

"Who is that?"

The dowager bent forward in her turn to the left, and the movement was started as in a field of wheat, the white shoulders bent, and the same question, "Who is that?" flew from group to group until it reached Guillaumette de Rueil, whom the diplomat, dazzled by the brilliancy of the lights, was endeavouring to discover behind the dancers. She was seated in the midst of four friends of her age, leaning back a little in her armchair, listening to the laughter around her, a little absent-minded, and patting, with little strokes, the folds of embroidered tulle which veiled her pink satin gown. Suddenly the murmur, "Who is that?" which spread from place to place, reached her; with a supple movement she straightened up. All her friends followed the movement of her face, which was bent forward. She squinted her eyes for a second, then two dimples hollowed her cheeks and her dazzling teeth appeared between the smooth lips.

"Ah!" she cried, "it is my Uncle Rabelcourt!"

And gliding between the waltzers, who saw nothing, with outstretched hands, rosy and dimpled under the aureole of her fair hair, the saucy patch which marked the right dimple displaced by her smile and lifted by a line, like the point of her eyebrows, the corner of her eyes, her nostrils, the curve of her mouth, Guillaumette de Rueil, in the reflections of stuffs and mirrors, moving in step to the music of the slow waltz, came toward Monsieur de Rabelcourt, who stood motionless, already bent to kiss her hand, and who watched her come. She kissed him:

"What a charming surprise, Uncle!"

"I could not come sooner," said Monsieur de Rabelcourt rapidly and in an undertone; "business, important business affairs, detained me, but I did not wish to fail at the rendezvous, my dear child."

She replied in the most natural tone and without lowering her voice.

"I cannot believe my eyes; my uncle at Monant! Where do you come from?"

"Why, from Belgium, of course," murmured Monsieur de Rabelcourt; "you know very well."

"On purpose to see us?"

"Naturally."

"Then I take it for granted that you are going to stop with us?"

"I had Claude take my luggage up."

THE DIPLOMAT 139

"That is good of you. Édouard will be delighted!" And as she smiled, her blue eyes, still coaxing like those of a child, rested upon the old man; the latter gave an admiring toss of his head, thinking: "Marvellously well acted, Guillaumette! Not a change of countenance, not an avowal before witnesses! You belong to my race!"

Then, as the waltz stopped, and as all eyes were now turned toward Guillaumette de Rueil and toward him, Monsieur de Rabelcourt, who had been very serious until then, added with an unembarrassed air aloud:

"You are more Watteau than ever, Niece!"

"Do you think so?"

"Fresh and slim, quite the figure of a young girl!"

The smile on the lips of Madame de Rueil was accentuated. A droll thought must have been passing through her mind.

"Always the diplomat, Uncle!" she answered. "You have not changed either! Will you come with me? Édouard is in here."

As she spoke, she drew Monsieur de Rabelcourt into a small drawing-room where half a score of distinguished-looking country gentlemen, who had given up dancing, were playing cards. At the moment when Madame de Rueil entered, one of them turned around, laying his hand down on the table. He was tall and sinewy; his short-cropped hair was tinged with grey; his nose made an accentuated curve above his heavy moustache. In his soldierly face, which had but a limited number of simple expressions, with no intermediary shades, his first impulse could be read like an open book. He could not disguise an impression of annoyance, which Monsieur de Rabelcourt carefully noted, but quickly recovering himself, like a well-bred man, he rose and held out his hand:

"Is it possible, Uncle?" he said. "Your visits are so rare to us that, as you see, I am all astonishment. Are you on a mission in Berry?"

"Partially so, Nephew."

"I am delighted, because I hope that it will keep you with us."

"Oh, that depends; I am not yet settled, you understand."

Monsieur de Rabelcourt had said this, with his head up, his eyes fixed on those of Rueil, who tried to comprehend. But the young man did not try long, and half a minute later a stifled laugh told the players in the small drawing-room that the arrival of the uncle was not an unmixed source of delight to the nephew.

The diplomat was already mingling with the guests who crowded the adjoining room. Guillaumette presented him. They crowded around him. Some of the elderly ladies recognised him, having met him either at the famous fête of Monant, or at Paris. "The dear minister! Monsieur de Rabelcourt! How is it possible! Who could forget you! What a piece of luck for Berry! Do you remember the ball at the Austrian Embassy, at the end of the second Empire?"

Monsieur de Rabelcourt replied:

"Perfectly."

He remembered everything. He had ears for everybody, words for every one, and eyes for all the young women who bowed: "Madame de Hulle, Uncle; Madame de Houssy; Madame Guy Milet; Madame O'Parell; my dear friend Baroness de Saint-Saulge . . ." At the same time whispered words were interchanged behind him: "What did you say, my dear, a minister?" "Yes, plenipotentiary." "Ah! indeed, where?" "Formerly in America, I do not know precisely where." "Is he an entertaining man?" "Oh! extremely!"

Among the number, insidiously, according to his custom and without discouraging any advances, Monsieur de Rabelcourt chose the privileged ones whom he desired to group around him, retained them with a word, with a more attentive, more meaning glance, which said: "I will come back to you." He returned soon, in fact, after making the tour of the room, and as the dancing began, went to seat himself by the side of the Baroness de Saint-Saulge, who adjusted her train with a flattered smile. Two dowagers, not expressly invited, were on either side of her; a few quite young married women made a circle before them. Those less young and less ingenuous preferred to dance. Monsieur de Rabelcourt began by complimenting his neighbour in a very low tone, upon the fashion of her dress. The seven women leaned forward to gather the words of the former minister, and all brightened up. Then, feeling his words listened to, studied, master of his audience, feeling again that light shiver of ease which old birds must feel in the April sunshine, he began to converse. The history of the Jacobson concession had again a revival; they saw hammocks hung with blossoming bindweed reappear; Pepita, the Peruvian, whose name closes the lips for a double kiss; Juana, a "gloomy and jealous creature," besides others, whose memory skilfully mingled with the names of emperors, of presidents of faraway republics, of rivers and mountains, awoke in the youthful listeners of Monsieur de Rabelcourt an idea of diplomacy new to them. He told a story well and without hesitation, on account of the great experience which he had had with the same stories; he could lift his eyes beyond the little circle and note what took place in the two drawing-rooms. He noticed, for instance, that Madame de Rueil, invited three times in a brief space of time, had refused to dance and had placed herself at the piano. He remarked that she was a little flushed and agitated, that at times, leaning to the right of the keyboard, quite at the farther end of the room, she cast a glance as hostess on the group as if thinking: "My friends do not dance any more since uncle is here." The uncle thought: "She is troubled." That did not prevent him from talking; phrases followed each other from the mouth of Monsieur de Rabelcourt as music from the piano, equally fluent, full of the same light, commonplace, and measured gaiety.

Rather quickly they produced the inevitable weariness of ordinary music. The imprudent ones who had sought the neighbourhood of the diplomat became conscious that the latter took more pleasure in talking than they in listening;

they recognised that they were simply galvanising into life an old drawing-room success; that the only novelty in these stories of America was their names, that they had better ones in the Old World, and they regretted letting themselves be caught in the snare. One by one, they moved their chairs, enlarging the circle, sent their searching eyes around the great drawing-room, summoning help by a movement of the eyelids, let themselves be invited, and, excusing themselves with a pained gesture to Monsieur de Rabelcourt, departed waltzing away to return no more.

Only the two old ladies remained in the corner of the room, to whom Monsieur de Rabelcourt paid very little attention, but who expected still less, and the little Baroness de Saint-Saulge, a plain, angular woman of thirty-two, who pleased him by the natural insolence of her wit, the exuberance of her gestures, the flutelike tone of her voice, by the vengeance which she drew from her unattractiveness, in enduring, as if they were addressed to another, the most insistent glances and the most open flattery, and especially on account of the intimacy which he knew now existed between Madame de Rueil and this country neighbour. As an experienced tactician, he reflected that Guillaumette might conceal, or not tell all, while he had there, that evening, an unique occasion to get information, a witness, who could not be ignorant of anything, and who no doubt demanded nothing better than to be indiscreet. To question without betraying anything, to use vague words in the hope of attracting precise replies, to have the air of knowing everything in order to obtain a secret, such had been the classic process of Monsieur de Rabelcourt in public life. He resolved to use it again.

As soon as he felt himself alone, or nearly so, with Madame de Saint-Saulge, he turned away insensibly from the dowager on the right, made a change to the left, and leaning over the armchair in which the baroness was plunged, he said:

"I see with pleasure, Madame, that you are one of the best friends of my niece. The dear child has need of support!"

"Yes, we understand each other admirably well, although our dispositions are very different."

"There are circumstances," observed Monsieur de Rabelcourt sententiously, "which bring together the most opposite natures."

"We live very near each other," replied Madame de Saint-Saulge. "We knew each other before these last months, it is true, but we have been especially intimate during this long leave that Monsieur de Rueil has passed entirely at Monant. I come here, she comes to me, that is, they come. Yes, I am very fond of her, the poor darling, she is so good, so forgetful of herself!"

"You pity her, Baroness, since you say poor?"

"The term is applied as often to the rich! Who is there that has not his little troubles? Even the happiest, even Guillaumette?"

He bent a little lower and murmured:

"You know all, then — you, too?"

Madame de Saint-Saulge moved in her armchair slightly so as to re-establish the distance that

Monsieur de Rabelcourt was trying to lessen; she looked fixedly at the diplomat, asking herself: "What does he mean? What is he alluding to? I only know very simple things on the subject of this straightforward and very happy household. Let this old ferreter come to the point, and let us not make any advances!" She replied, therefore, in the most matter-of-fact tone, playing with the chain of her gold lorgnette, which she rolled upon the handle of her fan:

"What do you mean, Monsieur?"

"That Guillaumette, in the first place, seems preoccupied."

"I don't think so."

"She keeps looking at us, do you see?"

"Apparently, she is fond of both of us."

"She does not dance!"

"That is—quite natural."

"No, Madame, it is not natural, she used to adore dancing—she is suffering. Do not try to deceive me! I have guessed the wrong which has been done her, the abandonment, the neglect, poor child!"

Madame de Saint-Saulge gave a start, she raised her eyes eagerly, which had been following the courtesies of the eight dancers in the minuet, and took her lorgnette the better to gaze at Monsieur de Rabelcourt. In the glance with which she scanned the troubled face of her interlocutor there beamed all her amused youth, her great contempt for the shrewdness of men, her delight in finding an opportunity of ridiculing a diplomat, the roguishness of the child persisting and living in the woman of thirty. Inclining her head a little, delighted to feel contempt for Monsieur de Rabelcourt:

"Do you allude to their intimacy?" she asked.

"Precisely."

"It is very great."

"I was sure of it!" said Monsieur de Rabelcourt, growing bolder. "I guessed it by certain signs! But what a sad thing, Madame, and improbable!"

"Improbable? No, I expected it and others with me, everybody——"

She smiled. He assumed a still more serious air to add:

"Indeed? Does the neighbourhood suspect something?"

"It is only a suspicion, still vague. It is so recent!"

"Two months perhaps?"

"Assuredly not more than three," said Madame de Saint-Saulge, laughing outright.

"I envy you, Madame," said Monsieur de Rabelcourt, "that you can speak of such a situation with so much indifference. You are not, like myself, bound by close ties of relationship with Guillaumette. Tell me, has she reproached her husband? Have there been scenes?"

"About that, I know nothing!" answered the young woman, opening her fan. "No one can know anything of that—you ask me for details of an intimacy——"

"So much the better, a thousand times better, Madame! I am glad that there is no scandal.

A mere murmur in the vicinity. My niece is so proud that she has concealed everything. People do not reproach her, I hope, for the slightest fault?"

"What do you mean?"

"I mean that Édouard is the only one at fault and that is just what I thought!"

"Why, no, Monsieur, he is not!"

"You absolve him?"

"Certainly! An accomplished man, serious and gay, a charming man whom every one likes!"

"She is the one," thought Monsieur de Rabelcourt. He rose severe and incapable of restraining his indignation.

"Madame," he murmured, "you are very young, but even at the risk of appearing to you to belong to the iron or stone age, I must think Monsieur de Rueil's conduct unqualifiable."

The Baroness de Saint-Saulge, struggling with a mad desire to laugh, replied after a moment:

"What a droll dictionary you have, Monsieur!"

"It is not a question of dictionaries, Madame, it is the foundation even of our feelings which differs—completely—completely."

He bowed, and the young woman followed with her eyes, in which the smile had died, this singular uncle, whom she had not yet catalogued in her rich collection of worldly souvenirs.

It was warm. The evening lacked animation after the arrival of this inconvenient personage, who seemed to monopolise the attention of Madame de Rueil from the distance and that of Madame de Saint-Saulge near by. It dragged on for half an hour more, until refreshments were served, then the noise of carriages arriving one by one before the château made the window-panes rattle. The neighbours took leave with the usual: "Charming evening, adieu," which was not wholly so false as elsewhere. Madame de Saint-Saulge, on taking leave of her friend, whispered in her ear:

"What a delightful man your uncle is!"

"You think so?"

"It is impossible to be bored an instant with him. He has imagined a crazy story about you. I misled him, and we ended by abusing each other. I will come and tell you about it in the morning."

Guillaumette replied with her habitual calm smile:

"Do so, dear. Till to-morrow then."

And she remained in the drawing-room alone with Monsieur de Rabelcourt, while her husband accompanied a group of friends to the steps.

Scarcely was the door closed when Monsieur de Rabelcourt, seized again by the idea of his mission, approached his niece and, pressing her hands between both of his, said to her tragically, in hurried words:

"We have but a moment, Guillaumette. . . . I know enough. You will tell me the rest. We will act together, my poor child."

She did not seem to understand.

"But I have nothing to tell you, my dear Uncle!"

"Do not dissimulate. Nothing this evening, but to-morrow. You have sent for me?"

"No."

THE DIPLOMAT 149

"Your letter!"

Guillaumette de Rueil blushed to the roots of her fair hair. Embarrassed, hesitating, confused, she remained a moment without saying anything, asking herself if it were necessary or not to confide in her uncle, who had so little discretion, whom she had been wrong to alarm. She decided in the negative, and putting her two arms on the shoulders of the old man, smiling and caressing, she kissed him, saying:

"I wrote that in a moment of folly. You will know all some day soon, I promise you. Do not be alarmed at a trifle. I do not think now what I did when I wrote. . . . If you wish to give me pleasure——"

"Yes, certainly!"

"Then do not insist. Forget the letter. Above all, never allude to it before Édouard. He would be furious with me."

"Come, my dear Uncle," said Édouard de Rueil, coming in, "let us have a game of billiards, will you, it is only eleven o'clock!"

"I thank you, Nephew," said Monsieur de Rabelcourt coldly. "I feel the fatigue of one hundred and twenty-seven leagues of railway travel in my body and of many cares in my mind. May I ask you to ring for the valet, Guillaumette. I will retire."

A moment later, upon the first flight of the stairway, the very dignified Monsieur de Rabelcourt, followed by his enlarged shadow turning on the wall, mounted in placing his two feet on each step and by little jerky strides displaying the form and the elasticity of his calf. Before him, the valet carried the candle. In the large drawing-room, behind the half-closed door, Monsieur and Madame de Rueil were seized with a sudden fit of merriment, and the former said:

"What is the matter with him, with your worthy uncle, Guillaumette? I find him most depressing! Have you any idea why he has that manner with me?"

"Not yet. I will find out to-morrow."

"At least, I hope that he has not come to stay?"

"I hope——"

"You did not invite him?"

"Oh! Not exactly."

"Deliver me from him, I say! For our last days—that would be gay! We must go back to Limoges at the end of the week. If he remains here—well, I consider my leave already at an end."

She reflected a moment and said:

"I will find a way by sleeping on it."

He, accustomed to her having wit for two, looked at her with admiration, took her at her word, and, already relieved, said:

"Shall we go up, too?"

And they went, without valet and without formality.

III.

Monsieur de Rabelcourt slept little; the fatigue of the journey, the change of bed, and children's cries penetrating through the ceiling, from the nursery on the second floor, kept him awake a part of the night. He had time to make a plan of battle. In spite of all, his mind was rested; his ideas took shape of themselves; his old experiences counselled him without even hesitating on the way to act.

"I am in the presence of a very simple and well-known case. A wife has been betrayed. It is she. In the first moment of her indignation she seeks a deliverer, a man who may be a discreet confidant and a natural protector. That is myself. This friend, this relative hastens to her; she loses her head at the thought of completing the avowal, of analysing herself, her wrong; she hesitates through modesty, through fear also of the necessary consequences and of the explanation which has not taken place, the anger, the probable separation. What must he do? Firstly, remain so as to add to the proofs which he possesses already, and secondly, as soon as he has his file of papers complete lay it before this too weak woman, say to her paternally: 'I have no need of admission; the proof is obtained; let us act!'"

At the hour of the early breakfast he found the family assembled in the dining-room. The children were all ready for company in immaculate frocks, seated, according to size, by the side of their mother; Jean and Pierre in blue, Louise in pink, little Roberte, supported by her mother's arms, standing tottering in her wool socks.

"Good morning, Uncle!" Three fresh voices saluted Monsieur de Rabelcourt, who came in, three smiles welcomed him, followed him as he approached, and were effaced when the absorbed and not very paternal uncle gave to each child, as a reward, a little tap on the cheek.

"Are they not darlings?" asked Guillaumette. "Whom do they resemble?"

"My dear," replied Monsieur de Rabelcourt, "I never judge women before twenty or men before thirty."

He pressed the hand of Édouard de Rueil, who half rose from the chair where he was seated and said:

"Well, Uncle, have you your plans for to-day?"

"Always, Nephew."

"I will wager that one is to see again Madame de Saint-Saulge. You know you paid her the most assiduous attentions last evening. Confidences, affected airs, discreet laughs, nothing was lacking."

"Except perhaps sympathy," answered Monsieur de Rabelcourt, seating himself before his cup of chocolate.

"What do you say!" cried Guillaumette, who was fastening the napkin behind Roberte's neck. "Thérèse did not please you? She charms every one!"

Monsieur de Rabelcourt cast a pitying glance on her, as on a child who does not comprehend, and fixing his gaze on Monsieur de Rueil, who looked up a little astonished from the opposite side of the table:

"A giddy-head!" he said.

"A woman full of good sense, full of heart," said Édouard.

"You are not mistaken on the last point, Monsieur de Rueil. I believe that she has enough for two." He laughed one of his laughs, which he termed sardonic, but which was like all the others.

"Your best friend?" he added.

"Certainly."

"Guillaumette told me so, Madame de Saint-Saulge confirmed it, and you repeat it. I have not the least doubt, but I think that Guillaumette might have chosen better. This intimate friend," he emphasised the epithet, "talked to me in a way . . ."

"Frivolous, Uncle?" interrupted Monsieur de Rueil, whose strong, stern countenance beamed with satisfaction. "You must have challenged it then. I know you; you are a hermit, but not a strict one. Confess now that you told some tales of South America to Madame de Saint-Saulge."

"No, Monsieur, the stories came from her. They were stories of this country, of your neighbourhood, of your immediate neighbourhood."

He paused to judge of the effect of his words, which did not appear to be considerable. And raising his voice, flushed, his lips tightly pressed, Monsieur de Rabelcourt added:

"Without insisting further for the present, I repeat to you that she flaunted before me an easy code of morality, more than easy. . . . I make no pretensions to being a model, but between her code of morals and mine, Heaven be praised, there is an abyss."

"My dear Uncle," exclaimed Guillaumette,

troubled at the turn the conversation was taking, "I assure you that you are mistaken. She must have been joking. She is bright and she loves controversy. When you become better acquainted, you will see that the abyss is a very shallow ditch."

"You are blind," said Monsieur de Rabelcourt. "But Monsieur de Rueil should understand me better. I would prefer to see your baroness ten leagues from here."

"Speak for yourself!" said Rueil, who was getting irritated.

"I speak for you, on the contrary; for you personally," said Monsieur de Rabelcourt. "I would rather see her a hundred leagues from here than in your house."

"Madame la Baronne de Saint-Saulge would like to speak to madame," announced the valet, opening the door. "I have shown her into the small drawing-room."

Guillaumette de Rueil, after an instant of surprise, recalled the rendezvous made the evening before; and leaning over her four besmeared children who had finished their breakfast without breathing a word:

"My darlings," she said, "you must ask your great-uncle for his most beautiful story of America. You are going to see how good they are, Monsieur le Ministre!" she added, laughing. "Spoil them for ten minutes, and do not malign my friend behind my back; that would be to betray her."

She cast a glance full of prudent recommendations to her husband, to which Édouard de Rueil

replied by a shrug of the shoulders, which said:
"I will be silent, but do not leave me long with
your uncle; he exasperates me."

She crossed the room and went out. Monsieur
de Rabelcourt looked at his nephew fixedly, finished his chocolate without saying another word,
and went up to his room.

Édouard de Rueil did not detain him.

IV.

After five minutes' conversation the two young
women rose and kissed each other. There were
tears in the eyes of Madame de Rueil. The other
was laughing.

"You are silly, Guillaumette, to cry because
your uncle is not a good psychologist."

"To suspect my husband! To invent such a
story! To talk about it at a ball in my house!
To assume the appearance of a judge before
Édouard, who has not a fault, whom I love, whom
I— You must admit that?"

"Why did you write to him?"

"I did not know what I was about."

"Then tell all to your husband."

"He will be angry with me. He will think me
silly, and he will be right. And yet, if I do not
say anything, we shall have a family scene, Rabelcourt against Rueil."

"Do better than that."

"What shall I do?"

"Turn Édouard over to me. I invite him for
breakfast. Everything is arranged; my carriage

is waiting at the end of the park; we will start at once, he and I; I will keep him until five o'clock; that will give you time to bring your uncle to reason, and when they meet again there will be no more clouds to forge thunderbolts."

"Admirable! But say nothing about my letter?"

"I promise."

Guillaumette dried her eyes, crossed the room, half opened the dining-room door and pressing her head in the opening:

"Good news, Édouard," said she. "The house is untenable with this poor uncle, who seems to me more and more eccentric. Madame de Saint-Saulge has come to your rescue; she invites you to breakfast."

"I fly!" said Rueil. "Try to get rid of him. But what has he against me anyway?"

"I will explain that to you," said Madame de Saint-Saulge, taking him by the arm.

They went down the steps together, and Madame de Rueil watched them as they walked slowly down the sunny avenue leading toward the woods, which began half-way down the slope. Her parasol concealed Madame de Saint-Saulge's head, but the gay note of her laugh made itself heard. The officer shook his head as if to say: "It is not credible!" made gestures with his cane, bent down to hear what his neighbour was saying and the confidences must have been amusing, for they moderated their youthful pace. They made a pretty group: he, in a close-fitting suit of blue which revealed his tall form; she, dressed in a light billowy gown, striped with mauve, her long skirt trailing over the grass and sand, looked like a great white poppy. Guillaumette followed them with her glance through the window, and as they were about to reach the turn of the grove and to disappear under the trees, she observed her friend lift up her parasol, look for a second in the direction of the house and at once take a more rapid gait. Madame de Saint-Saulge was fleeing with her invited guest.

From whom?

The question was not long in being answered.

Coming out from the shadow of the right tower, passing between the central clump of vervains and the bunches of petunias which edged the turf, launched with all the swiftness which the rotundity of his figure permitted, Monsieur de Rabelcourt appeared. He was running in the same direction. His head which he held forward, his eyes fixed upon the end of the avenue, followed the fugitives. He had seen them from his room. Doubting his eyes, he had examined with his field-glass this pair of young people who were making their escape so resolutely and so gaily into the country. It was he! It was she! Monsieur had not an instant's hesitation. He seized his cane, hurried down-stairs, opened the door cautiously. He had sworn an oath to catch them; and with his whole power, he was striving to keep his word.

Madame de Rueil guessed that the promenaders were hastening their pace on his account. But she hesitated to believe that her uncle was trying to overtake them. For a moment she watched the lessening silhouette of Monsieur de Rabelcourt. Soon doubt was no longer possible. "Good gracious!" she thought, "he is chasing them!"

She opened the window and called:

"Uncle, Uncle!"

He did not hear, or pretended that he did not. His shoulders twisting, his legs, which described unusual curves, raising a cloud of dust at each step, his silk hat shaken by the run, he continued on the way to the sheltered paths in which Madame de Saint-Saulge and Édouard de Rueil had just disappeared.

Guillaumette wished for a horse, a bicycle, for wings to fly after him, to stop him, to prevent a scene. Agitated, anxious, unable to think how to prevent the meeting of the adverse parties, she caught her garden hat, pinned it quickly on her head, and, taking a path which crossed the lawn and reached the woods on the right, she plunged into the thicket, to meet her uncle at least on his return from the other end of the park, by the most direct path.

She, too, walked very quickly. She seated herself on a bench, in an opening where three diverging paths, full of quivering shadows rocked by the wind, could be seen. Madame de Rueil listened, her ear strained toward the distance below, in which this chase of a diplomat running down an intrigue in flight was continuing. After some moments she heard a voice deadened by the distance and the leaves. The voice was raised three times and, although the words could not be dis-

tinguished, it was clear that they were violent
and that they commanded. Then silence ensued;
the woods were asleep in the heat. In the cut-
tings and thickets around Monant, you felt this
long shivering of twigs, which the ear confounds
with silence and which, at certain hours, grows
faint like the roar of the sea, diminish and die
gradually.

Ten minutes passed; suddenly Madame de
Rueil waved her parasol, signalling:

"Here I am! Come!"

Monsieur de Rabelcourt emerged from the end
of a green path. He saw his niece. He was
walking with a less rapid gait than on leaving the
château, but it was still nervous and strained.
He appeared to be carrying on a lively conversation with himself; he twirled his cane, now and
then cutting off shoots of brambles; he raised
his shoulders, straightening up as if an adversary
were before him. As soon as he came in reach of
her voice, Madame de Rueil cried to him:

"Did you overtake them?"

"Yes."

She turned pale; he drew near.

"What did you do then? Uncle, I am so dis-
tressed! What did you do?"

"My duty!"

He was flushed and panting, still filled with
the pride of his victory; but there was pity mingled with it for this young wife, who was watching him come from the distance, and was so
troubled. Monsieur de Rabelcourt stopped near
her and said:

"Do not be alarmed, my poor darling! Do not be agitated; let me relate the affair from the beginning."

But she drew him to her, moved aside a little and made him sit down near her:

"Quick, quick, tell me, on the contrary, what has just happened. I am so unhappy! It is all my fault—I ought to have explained my letter to you—you did not understand it——"

"Everything, my child, everything!"

"No, you did not!"

"Let me speak. You will see. But don't interrupt me any more! Yes, your letter gave me the first suspicion, almost the certainty. I hasten to Monant; I find you agitated; I see your husband annoyed at my coming; I question Madame de Saint-Saulge, she confesses——"

"What? Since there is nothing."

"She confesses this betrayal from which you are suffering, unhappy child, and which you wish to hide from me now!" resumed Monsieur de Rabelcourt, raising both arms. "She avowed it with perfect cynicism to me, your uncle, in your house! Ah! I did not miss her just now! I saw your husband with her in the path, I ran after them. Anger restored my youth, I did not catch up with them, for they almost ran, but I got near enough for my voice to carry, and——"

"Great heavens, what did you say?"

"I cried at the top of my lungs: 'Monsieur de Reuil, you are betraying your most sacred duties, but hereafter there is a witness; I am the one!'"

"What did he do? Was he angry?"

"No."

"At least, he replied very sharply?"

"Not at all. In place of stopping, he went on running; he merely looked over his shoulder and threw this simple impertinence at me: 'Au revoir, you old sheep!' while his accomplice, still more giddy than he, hurried him along; I heard them laughing, Guillaumette, laughing after they were out of sight!"

"Ah! so much the better! So much the better!"

She could not utter another word. Tears, nervous agitation, the rebound of the emotion which she had felt, prevented her from speaking; half turned toward Monsieur de Rabelcourt, she made a sign with her lashes, with her lips lifted at the corners, with all her pretty fair head, and said: "Do not mind me, I was afraid, I was faint for a moment, but I am happy, enchanted, pleased, and I will explain!"

Monsieur de Rabelcourt thought her out of her senses. He looked at her in silence, he studied the changing play of her face and her expressions which were effaced one after the other; he felt some anxiety and remorse in the presence of his niece as one does before one of those pretty, fragile toys whose spring you have unintentionally snapped, without knowing how to mend it.

She mended herself all alone.

Suddenly, Madame de Rueil stopped crying; she seized both her uncle's hands and became grave, affectionate even. Having recovered her frank expression, she said:

"My dear Uncle, it is my fault, but you have made a grievous mistake!"

At that moment, she resembled so greatly personified reason, she had such an air of conviction, that he lost his. Monsieur de Rabelcourt felt that he had blundered, and blushed beforehand for what he was going to learn.

"What mistake, Guillaumette?" he demanded.

"Are you not unhappy?"

"I was for twenty-four hours. I am not so any longer."

"Has not your husband deceived you?"

"He is the most faithful and the most loving of husbands!"

"I did not, however, dream my conversation with Madame de Saint-Saulge?"

"It was a joke!"

"She spoke to me of an intimacy of Édouard's?"

"With me."

"She has just taken him home with her."

"With my full consent; he breakfasts at Roches."

"Then, why the devil did you call me?"

"I did nothing of the kind!"

"Oh! indeed! What do you call your letter?"

"My dear Uncle," said Guillaumette, in her sweetest voice, "you must not get angry with me; you have too much experience not to know that even the happiest of young women have moments when they detest life, when their youth is no consolation to them, indeed, quite the contrary. I went through one of these crises. My letter was written by your Guillaumette, already burdened with rather a large family!——"

THE DIPLOMAT 163

"Jean, Pierre, Louise, Roberte," counted the uncle.

"In six years," she resumed. "The mother wished for a little liberty, a little vacation. She had the disagreeable surprise——"

"You are?"

"Yes, Uncle; a little fifth!"

"With your slim figure!"

"We will baptise it at Limoges, this winter."

"And that is all your trouble!"

"It is quite enough! Do not get angry!"

"And you had the face to write to me for such a little thing that you would like to start with me for Buenos Ayres?"

"I was sorry for it the next day."

"And you gave me three weeks of distress by explaining nothing to me! You make me take a journey of one hundred and twenty-seven leagues; I arrive, I believe that you are betrayed, I suspect Madame de Saint-Saulge, I offend your husband, I risk making trouble between two households, and I seriously compromise my reputation as a man of the world and a diplomat, and when the evil is done, you mean to tell me that all this fine despair came to you from what is called a hope! Really, my dear, it is unpardonable!"

Monsieur de Rabelcourt drew away his hands, which, until then, Guillaumette de Rueil had retained in her own, and, offended, straightening up against the back of the bench, he began to look vaguely at the forest trees.

The young wife did not try to defend herself,

she felt that she was at fault; but, remembering the recommendations of Édouard and the time which was passing, she tried to find out the intentions of Monsieur de Rabelcourt. From the other end of the bench, her eyes vague also and dreamy, she said:

"I take it upon myself to reconcile you with Madame de Saint-Saulge."

He made no answer.

"The most difficult thing will be," she continued, "to make my husband listen to reason. He will pardon you, Uncle, without any trouble!—but it will be necessary to confess to him that I wrote that peevish, ridiculous letter. And I am so worried. He will be only too much disposed to think as you, that I had no sense on that day in not keeping silent, and that I had less yesterday evening in keeping silent.—He is so good to me that his reproaches are infinitely hard for me."

Monsieur de Rabelcourt let her continue her monologue without interrupting her.

At the end of a quarter of an hour, he sighed, his features relaxed, he looked at his niece with eyes in which there was much indulgence and a little regret.

"Come!" said he, "let us return to the château. I will make the explanation very easy for you. Fear nothing. Are you able to walk back?"

Both rose. As they were going up the steps, Monsieur de Rabelcourt, who had recovered his good humour more from moment to moment, added:

"All the same, the trip will not have been with-

THE DIPLOMAT 165

out benefit for me. It will have recalled to me what we men are always tempted to forget, that one should never hurry to help a woman who complains. Order the horse to be harnessed, my little Guillaumette."

Some moments later, as the victoria, which was used to go from Monant to the neighbouring station, was carrying away Monsieur de Rabelcourt and turning the corner of the château, the diplomat put his head out of the carriage, completely restored to serenity, already smiling at the shadows of Wimerelles, and bowing to his niece, who was leaning out of a low window, he cried:

"Good-bye, Guillaumette, good-bye! Do not disturb me for the sixth!"

THE WILL OF OLD CHOGNE.

THE WILL OF OLD CHOGNE.

NOTHING told the hour, unless it was the silence. It must have been near midnight, or a little after the dead point of the dial, in that brief period, when the very watch-dogs rouse themselves with difficulty. Only at long intervals there came a brief lowing from the stable, the cry of an animal exhausted by the accumulated heat which the snow on the roof kept stored. No noise; no light either in the great room of the farm. There were two men, however, seated near the table on which the masters and servants of the Beinost Farm ate their morning and evening meals, both on the same side and looking at the bed, whose motionless clothes and coverlid were raised their whole length by a human form. Around the bed, on the right of the fireplace, the sheets dragged on the floor; other sheets were drying, stretched on the back of a chair, in front of the scattered logs which were growing grey with ashes. Elsewhere, along the walls of the room, as in all farmhouses of the region, there was a provision of wood carefully piled up, a dish-closet, a clothes-press crowned with boots with widened tops, a chest, two or three sacks of potatoes or chestnuts. These objects emerged from the shadows very vaguely. The reflections from the fields of snow, which do not lose all light at night, entered through the panes of opposite windows and kept, for the accustomed eyes of the witnesses, somewhat of the life of colours and of outlines. At last the men spoke in an undertone.

"He has not budged for an hour," said one.

"I do not hear his breath any longer," replied the other.

"He passed away so suddenly," resumed the elder, "that there was not time to have him make his will. It can't be, however, that Mélanie should share with us in father's property."

"No, that mustn't be! The meadow must be ours, and the vineyard below too, and the whole Farm."

"Then you agree with me, Francis?"

"Yes."

"Entirely?"

The younger replied with a nod, accompanied by a lowering of the eyelids, which signified: "I know what I have to do; it is useless to talk." He was young, thin, and colourless, with yellow hair, an aquiline nose, and light-coloured, continually shifting eyes. Some people took him for a creature of little judgment; they did not notice the brief laugh which barely stretched his lips and cheeks, but in which a resolute and cunning spirit was shown.

Anthelme, the elder, a heavy, bearded, thick-faced, and flat-nosed peasant, gave one the impression of brutal and impelling strength, but he had his share of cunning too, which he cloaked under the violence of words, tone, and gesture. Habitually, people heard only of him at the Beinost Farm. The real master was, however, the father, who had just died and after him the younger son, who was like his father. Francis was the first to rise.

"Go and fetch Biolaz," he said; "I will get the witnesses and arrange the rest."

A quarter of an hour later the great black mare, whose mouth, drawn too early by the bit, had remained stretched as if by a stupid laugh, waited, in the snow, in the farmhouse court. Francis stood by the sleigh; he had a last injunction to give, and when the stable door opened, he said:

"Anthelme, don't talk too much with Biolaz!"

He went in immediately, shaking his jacket. Anthelme had wrapped himself up in a lined carter's coat, a wretched cloak which had been used for twenty years by all the cowherds of the Farm, and his head almost disappeared in the funnel of the high collar. He came forward carrying before him the lighted lantern, which he fastened in an iron ring on the right of the seat, and then he started. The mountain was entirely white, without tree or bush as far as the first fields of the valley. He tried, therefore, in the radiance of the slopes, to recognise the path, which he could not leave without risking his life. The snow was falling softly. The villages, below, in the icy fog, were asleep. No sound came up from the valleys. Nothing was moving, in that winter's night, unless it were, very high up on the

Colombier, the flame of the lantern, which made around the sleigh a tiny halo which went down in zigzags across the fields of snow.

Anthelme Chogne was going to fetch the notary. These Chognes were known in the mountain as a rich, litigious family, at all times to be feared by those who were not of use to them. It was a saying among the neighbours: "One never does a good stroke of business with a Chogne, and those are lucky even who do not do a bad one." The old father rarely came down from his farm, perched some two thousand feet up in the air, in the bulky part of the Colombier, where the peaks diminish in size and where the mountain spreads out its sides. When summer had melted the snows, one saw nothing around the Beinost Farm but poor pasture-lands strewn with stones and unfenced fields where the surface of the soil, scratched by the plough and spade, gave back meagre harvests of rye, beans, and potatoes; but below, upon an old marsh, bordered by a torrent, there was a vineyard, shaped like a turtle, which gave a pale-red, piquant wine very celebrated in the neighbourhood. This vineyard was the pride and the wealth of the Chognes. There was besides, above the farm, a pine forest, rising up dark and crowded together to the summit of the chain, which did not belong to the Chognes, but which they, from father to son, exploited and devastated with an audacity against which the owner had never found any valid defence. Did trees disappear? No one had ever seen the woodcutter who cut them down. Were they found

OLD CHOGNE

at the foot of the mountain, in the fold, where the trunks of trees run whether borne down by avalanches or by the torrent? The Chognes always claimed that the wood belonged to them, that it came from a cutting on the outskirts bought by them, and proof against them was impossible in this vast and sparsely populated country, difficult of access and where no witness would dare to say: "Chogne lies." Father Chogne, of a morose, avaricious disposition, had never willingly tolerated the presence of a woman in his house. His only daughter, Mélanie, grown stupid from want of care and lack of nourishment, at the age of fifteen had taken a place as servant at Nantua. She was now twenty-five years old, and it was she whom it was necessary to despoil of the vineyard and the Farm, and of all that the father would have taken away from her if he had not died so suddenly on that winter's night.

Anthelme put the mare to a trot on reaching the plain. He passed hamlets, one after another, without stopping, and barely slackened his speed in going up the slope on the other side of the valley to reach the pass which joins Valromey with Hauteville. The snow was soft and very deep on the heights. Fortunately it had ceased to fall in this region. The sleigh glided along a wide road marked out by forests or clusters of trees. The second descent was easy and rapid. The peasant stopped about the middle of the principal street of the town, before a door to which you mounted by four steps, provided with a balustrade; he threw the blanket over the mare, whose body smoked like a pool at dawn.

"Hullo now, Monsieur Firmin Biolaz!" he cried, pulling the bell at the same time. A sharp and prolonged peal answered him, a trembling of copper wire, which died away slowly and without result. It was only at the third call that the blinds of the first floor, lightly pushed upon their iron hinges, let a white nightcap appear which waved in the air, and a voice demanded:

"Can't you ring a little less hard? Who are you?"

"I am come to get you for a will."

"Is it urgent?"

"Yes, very."

"Then I will go in the morning. Who are you?"

"In the morning! No, that will be too late! You must come at once. Everything is ready."

The man raised his voice so that he might have been heard even to the depths of the alcoves where the neighbours were sleeping behind their drawn curtains.

"Open the door, Monsieur Biolaz; the law says that notaries cannot refuse clients! Open!"

The blinds drew together. Then Anthelme heard the muffled noise of the paddings of the window as it closed. He remained outside only long enough for the notary to light a candle, explain to his wife that there was no danger, put on his slippers, draw on his trousers, tuck in the ample folds of his nightshirt, and come downstairs.

"Come in quick," said Monsieur Biolaz; "it is devilishly cold."

"That is no news to me!"

"This way," said the notary, pushing open, on the left of the corridor, the door of his office. He went in first, pushed forward a chair, in the darkness disturbed by the flickering candle, walked around the desk, and seated himself in his accustomed place, lifting up the flat candlestick to study his client. The latter unbuttoned the collar of his coat, drew out his beard, upon which bits of melting snow were running, took off his cap, and announced:

"I am Chogne, Anthelme Chogne of the Beinost Farm."

"Chogne!" repeated the notary, setting down the candlestick. "Ah, very well! Who, then, is sick at your house?"

"The old man; he will not live through the night; that is certain."

"Very well, very well," repeated the notary. The two men observed each other during a half-minute of silence, each seeking to read and not to be read. The faces remained fixed, inexpressive; nevertheless, by the direct communication, which is always established between two minds in conflict, Anthelme understood, he plainly saw, that Monsieur Biolaz thought: "All these Chognes are rascals; let us be on our guard." Monsieur Biolaz, on his side, knew to a certainty that Anthelme Chogne of the Beinost Farm thought: "The notary has heard people talk about us; he does not think very well of us, but I am shrewder than he." This man, still young and thick-set, recalled by his spotted red face, his drooping eyelids and the nervous twitch which drew down one corner of his lips, his regulation short-cropped hair, and his awkward movements, the legendary type of foot-soldier just entering the barracks; but he had always lived in the country and he had fathomed what he termed *"la clinique notariale."* He demanded:

"Can you get witnesses at this hour of the night?"

"They will be at the Farm, all four, when you get there. Come on!"

The peasant's neck swelled out; his eyes became bloodshot; he struck the table with his fist.

"Come on! Will you finally decide to go?"

Monsieur Biolaz had a fluttering of the eyelids and a kind of assent of the head which Anthelme took for a sign of fear. He made no answer, but he rose, seized a bag hanging upon the green wall-paper, and slipped some legal cap, some stamped paper, some pens in it, and, at the last moment, an object contained in a rectangular leather case, as high as your hand, which stood on the desk.

"You don't need to take your revolver, you know!" said Anthelme in a jeering tone. "The house is safe."

The notary snapped the spring which closed his bag.

"Pass first, Monsieur Chogne; I am not taking a revolver, it is a small instrument with which I take notes, when I need them."

Anthelme did not have long to wait in the street. Monsieur Biolaz reappeared, in high boots, wrapped in a goatskin, dragging a fur covering after him; he wrapped himself up in these furs, stretched himself in the back of the sleigh, without making an observation or a remark, his bag under his head, and murmured:

"At your service, Monsieur Chogne!"

During the greater part of the way and until he had reached the foot of the mountain, near his vineyard, Anthelme appeared to have no other preoccupation than that of urging his already jaded mare to a gallop. The sudden change of speed when the ground rose restored speech to the driver. Anthelme turned half around upon the seat of the sleigh. He recognised by the shapes which the mist was taking that daylight was approaching, and that the morning would be clear.

"Monsieur Biolaz, do you know my father well?"

"I have met him once or twice at fairs."

"He will certainly recognise you; he has a good memory! I say, Monsieur Biolaz, do you know my brother Francis well?"

"Not at all."

The peasant whipped up his exhausted mare, adding:

"Perhaps he will be there and perhaps he will not. He went for the doctor for father, you see."

They were watching for the travellers at the Beinost Farm, and as soon as the sleigh drew up before a kind of platform which extended behind the farmhouse the door of the great hall opened and a man came out in the darkness, saying:

"Welcome! Come in quickly! He is still alive, but you must be quick; he moans continually."

The notary entered. The room was lighted only by a stable lantern of convex glass, which was placed in the centre of the table. He saw the bed, but all he could see of the sick man, hidden among the pillows and sheets, was a cotton night-cap and an indistinct profile turned toward the wall, from which there came an uninterrupted moan. The notary walked around the room and stopped by the fireplace among the chairs loaded with linen. The bed-curtains were half closed.

"It is I, Monsieur Chogne, it is I, the notary. Do you hear me well?"

A muffled voice replied:

"Yes, yes, Monsieur Biolaz of Hauteville. Oh, dear, dear! My dear sir, how sick I am!"

"Not so sick as you think, Monsieur Chogne. . . . Look at me."

Several voices from the rear of the room protested:

"Let him be. . . . He is sick enough as it is. Since he does not want to move, why disturb the man?"

They heard the drawling voice of the notary:

"Hand me the lantern."

The words fell in a silence as profound as if they had been uttered in the midst of fields of snow and the fog of dawn. Monsieur Biolaz repeated them with the same tranquil tone. Then the man who had come out to meet him in the court, a very tall man, with his hat pulled down over his eyes, seized the lantern by the copper

OLD CHOGNE

handle and lifted it up without leaving the middle of the room. Monsieur Biolaz did not insist; but he looked at the testator, who began again to moan, bending down over him; then he turned briskly away. In the back of the room, upon a bench along the wall, three other peasants were listening, and watching, scarcely breathing, their heads and shoulders bent forward. The movement of the notary made them start like persons caught in a fault. One of them cried ill-humouredly:

"Ply your trade, Monsieur Biolaz, instead of swinging yourself about like that in your goatskin."

The notary hesitated no longer; he had the feeling that he was alone against five, for Anthelme came in, after having unharnessed the mare, and said:

"That is so; bring your papers over to the lantern, Monsieur Biolaz; you can see there to write. Unfortunately we have no more oil; it has all been used these last days, you understand."

Then, as Monsieur Biolaz began asking the names, surnames, and trades of the witnesses, he continued:

"It is a pity that my brother Francis is not back in time for father's will; that will be a grief to him for his whole life."

The notary appeared to be no longer listening; he was drawing up the will. Spreading a sheet of stamped paper where the light of the lantern shone on it, he applied himself, his forehead creased with a single wrinkle, to combining his phrases and weighing his words. The witnesses became expansive. They chatted with each other.

"In the presence of Monsieur Firmin Biolaz, appeared Monsieur Mathieu Napoléon Chogne, who, believing himself to be mortally ill, requested the said Monsieur Biolaz to draw up his will." The notary put down afterward, with minutiæ, the circumstances of date and place, describing the hall of the Beinost Farm and the sick man himself, "as far as I could see him," he wrote. He then asked the testator to dictate his wishes to him. Old Chogne, whose speech was interrupted by frequent sighs, groans and fits of coughing, dictated, however, some phrases which revealed a long experience in business. He bequeathed, "as preference legacy and besides their share, to his sons Anthelme and Francis, all that he could will away from his daughter Mélanie, and this in gratitude for the good care with which they had surrounded his old age." He expressed the wish, "which should be sacred for all," that the vineyard should belong to Francis and the Beinost Farm to Anthelme. The drawing of the will concluded, Monsieur Biolaz read the deed aloud and rose to have the sick man sign. Two of the four witnesses and Anthelme rose at the same time, going between the notary and the bed. The two others crowded in the little space back of the bed.

"I cannot sign," groaned the sick man; "I am not able."

"Don't torment him again! You hear what he says," grumbled the men. "Monsieur Biolaz,

it must be written on the deed that he is not able
to sign. Monsieur Biolaz, do not go near him
like that; he is afraid of you, you see. Leave the
lantern on the table, the light hurts his eyes."

The notary was at the foot of the bed, which
was hidden by a covering reaching down to the
floor. The men on both sides of the sick man
moved about, bending over so closely to speak
to him that his face could not be seen.

"Isn't it true, old father, that you cannot sign?
Say it again. The notary must go now. Sick
persons like him, Monsieur Biolaz, should not be
annoyed."

During this time, the notary raised cautiously,
and without their noticing, the covering upon
which he had stepped. He had felt, through the
wool, something resisting and soft at the same
time; he had followed the contour with the tip
of his boot, and without for a single instant lowering
his eyes.

Had not the witnesses and Anthelme been so
intently occupied in shielding old Chogne, they
would have noticed Monsieur Biolaz turn pale.
The notary turned his head toward the window,
which was quite clear. The daylight without,
clear and made brighter by the snow, was coming
into the room. He moved back.

"Gentlemen, I will add the legal formula; I
will write that the testator is unable to sign.
Come, let us finish."

At once they resumed their places, all confronting
him on the other side of the table. He wrote
the phrase with his right hand; with his left, he

searched in the travelling-bag, taking the little box out of its case, which he placed standing on the top of the table.

"What are you going to do with that?" cried Anthelme. "I do not permit! . . . Prevent him!"

"It is I who will not permit you to hinder the witnesses from signing! Help, witnesses."

The witnesses put the struggling Anthelme aside; Monsieur Biolaz, turning the box toward the bed, pressed a noiseless spring, then hid the object in the pocket of his goatskin coat.

At this instant the elder of the Chognes bounded to the bed, bent down, pulled to the floor the covering which had been raised, and still crouching, his fists clinched, sought with a glance for the companion who would help him commit a crime. They could easily have thrown themselves on Monsieur Biolaz, searched him, bound him if he had resisted; but the notary seemed so self-possessed, so entirely occupied in arranging the signatures, that the eyes to which Anthelme appealed replied with an expressive look: "It is useless; he has seen nothing; do not compromise everything!"

"Imbeciles!" exclaimed Anthelme aloud, straightening himself up and taking his place as sentry at the foot of the bed.

Monsieur Biolaz said simply: "Anthelme, the first witness will take me home. Have another horse harnessed to the sleigh."

No one would have guessed, when the notary stretched himself, for the second time, in the wooden cage which was to carry him back to

OLD CHOGNE

Hauteville, that, in the same hour, he had discovered one crime and committed another.

The interment of old Chogne took place the second day after. On the fifth day, early in the morning, the two sons presented themselves at the office of Biolaz. The notary was expecting their visit. He seated them before his desk and remained standing on the other side. He had his usual naïve air and drawling tone, but his lips twitched more nervously than usual.

"Well, what do you want of me?" he asked.

He knew very well.

"We want to know whether you have had the will recorded," replied the elder.

"For my sister Mélanie agrees to all that father wished," added the younger; "she will not contest the will."

Monsieur Biolaz collected himself, dropped his eyelids very low, turned his eyes toward Anthelme's wolfish face, then toward Francis with his polecat nose, and, pausing between the words, said:

"The will has not been recorded, nor will it be; it is null!"

"Null!" cried Anthelme, pushing his chair back with violence. "It is not null. I saw it and I know what I am talking about!"

"You would have to prove its nullity!" added Francis.

The two brothers were standing leaning with their hands on the edge of the desk.

"Here is the document," said the notary, taking a sheet of paper, which they recognised. "It is thrice null. In the first place, you see this: 'who requested Monsieur Biolaz to draw up his will.'"

"Well?"

"There should have been put in also 'and dictated it.' The mention that the will was dictated is necessary. I omitted it."

"Purposely?"

"Yes."

"Scoundrel!"

"Wait, Anthelme, before calling names; we will see which of us three deserves it."

"What next, Monsieur Biolaz?" Francis asked.

"I neglected, in addition, to indicate that I read the will to the testator and witnesses; and lastly, and third nullity, I wrote, it is true, that the testator was too feeble to sign, but I did not state that he told me so himself."

The little sheet fell to the desk noiselessly as snow falls. The three men were seized by the same emotion, and their three angers met in the narrow space which separated their faces, arms, and chests.

"Own up, Biolaz," cried Anthelme, "in public documents, that is called forgery!"

"I know it."

"An act like that leads a man to the galleys!" exclaimed Francis.

"Certainly," answered Monsieur Biolaz, "such an act leads a public officer to the galleys, if he has not, in order to justify it, this little document here." He held out a small square brown paper. The two Chognes recoiled.

"Oh, you can take it; I have twenty similar proofs, and the plate is in a safe place."

It was the younger who took the print and carried it to the window. The proof was plain; the bed-curtains, the sheets, and the pillows were rounded up in hazy folds around a very typical but undecided profile, one without age. But in the foreground, at the spot where the window poured in the light more abundantly, beneath the bed, could be seen, could be distinguished, two white surfaces, spreading, joined, which ended by indentations.

"I have examined the plate with a magnifying-glass," said Monsieur Biolaz, "and there is no doubt that those are human feet, the feet of the dead, you understand, you two Chognes? The feet of your dead father, whom you had thrown under the bed!"

Anthelme and Francis did not turn round; they looked at each other, and in this look there was the command to Anthelme to keep silent, and the confession of a moment of confusion. Francis turned the print over, examined it, at close range and far off, to gain time. Finally he spoke:

"No one could swear that they were the feet of a dead person, Monsieur Biolaz. Neither would it be possible for any one to recognise the face in the bed; it is too small. No, there is no danger for us. But the world is so envious; these things would make a noise; people would talk about it. So then, my brother and I, we will let the will drop."

The notary made no reply; he pointed to the

door. They went out, but at the moment of parting, before going down the steps of the porch, Anthelme turned around and said, as if he were confiding a secret:

"You are sharp in your trade, Monsieur Biolaz, for all that; I do not say but that we may call upon you again just the same."

"Can't you hold your tongue?" cried Francis leading him away.

Monsieur Biolaz pushed the door and heard with satisfaction the click of the latch, which ended the visit.

THE LITTLE SISTERS OF THE POOR.

THE LITTLE SISTERS OF THE POOR.

I.

Père Honoré Le Bolloche, having no more work at all, came out of the shed where he worked, took a few steps outside and seated himself on the chair which he had just reseated; for he was by trade a chair-mender. First he stretched out his wooden leg, then the other, looked in his pouch for some tobacco, and, not finding any, felt that he was poor.

Poor, Le Bolloche had always been, but he had not always realised it, which constitutes, in the main, the true way of not being so. In the army, for instance, when he was sergeant of zouaves, what had he lacked? The handsomest man in the regiment, a long, bronzed face, with straight nose slightly flattened and widened at the base, an imperial which would have made more than one captain envious at that Napoleonic era when there were such decorative captains, shoulders thrown back, neck tanned and furrowed with white grooves, chest swelled out, he enjoyed the esteem of his comrades in arms and pay ample for his wants. His record bore to his debit only a few insignificant punishments for a few strong military outbreaks on glorious anniversaries: a hen snatched from the Bedouins; two or three too hasty retorts to his superiors, younger than he—mere trifles! The credit side was magnificent: five campaigns, all the chevrons possible, honourable mention in the order of the day, a military medal, a bugle for marksmanship, the small coin of a general in chief. Several times he had marched in triumph through towns, under arches of laurel, walking over flowers and applauded by women, on the return from Italy or from the Crimea. On those occasions he was put forward on account of his imposing bearing and certain wounds, which he had the wit to receive at favourable moments and in good places: a sabre cut on his temple at Solferino and a ball in the calf of his leg at Malakoff. Le Bolloche loved glory. Young soldiers, while admiring him, also credited him with a crabbed disposition, but his superior officers, better informed doubtless, declared that it was only his keen sense of honour. Heaven had given him a constitution proof against anything. Le Bolloche was happy.

Later even, struck by the age limit, according to his expression, he met after leaving the regiment with many pleasant experiences in this civil life which before he had daily abused. Accustomed to be commanded and to be surrounded by comrades, his liberty weighed upon him no less than his solitude. Still hale and hearty, and with agreeable manners besides, he had no difficulty in finding a wife. His wife was not very young, but he was beginning to grow old. She brought him, however, what passes for youth in the eyes of many people: a dot—a small house built on a low piece of ground beyond the *octroi*, a few square yards of meadow-land, or, to speak more clearly, two strips of grass on a slope, crossed in winter by a small stream of water, of which there remained in summer a round marsh large as a thrashing-floor.

The vicinity of the rushes growing there, the ignorance of any trade, and a certain deftness of hand were the reasons which led the old soldier to take up the trade of new-bottoming chairs. His prices were not excessive. Business came to him in plenty from the faubourg, where children took it upon themselves to give him work. He kept his health and for several years Le Bolloche had no reason to complain.

On the contrary, a joy, the greatest that he had ever known, came to him, and one of those which lasts: a child. He had wished more than anything for a daughter. The one his wife gave to him was rosy, fair, and gay. Le Bolloche recognised himself in her at once. It was an instant adoration. Although far from being a devout man, he wished to carry the child to church himself, and when the priest asked the name with which she was to be baptised—"Name her Désirée," he answered, "for I have never desired anything as much as I desired her." He took care of her and had more to do with raising her than the mother. When a mere baby, before she could walk even, she crept about in the shed while he worked.

She laughed and he was happy. If she cried he had wonderful ways of consoling her: he rocked her, sang to her like a nurse songs which have only three notes, like those that one hears in the trees at nesting time.

She had barely sense enough to keep still and strength enough to bend a rush before he taught her to braid cages, baskets, and boats, which they went to launch together on the pond. Later the amusement became an art. She soon knew all that her father knew and more besides. He was not jealous of this; he trusted to her the fine work, which demanded a deft hand, taste and invention. And whenever a bourgeois chair, that is, one not coarsely woven of rushes, but of fine rye straw, braided in one or two colours, was sent to the shop with a seat to be replaced or merely a break to be mended, Le Bolloche trusted it to Désirée. Raised tenderly in this way among three persons, who spoiled her to her heart's content, for Le Bolloche had brought his very old, blind mother home, it was scarcely possible that the child should not be amiable. In fact, a more comely girl could not be found in the whole faubourg or in the neighbouring country. She might have passed for a woman at fifteen. She was tall, well formed, rosy-cheeked, and slightly freckled. It was not that her eyes were longer or larger than another's, but that she looked so frankly at you that you divined in her a perfectly sincere nature.

She laughed readily, and her laugh lingered, like a fresh thing, in your memory. She did not wear a cap, partly from economy, still more to show her hair, rolled back from her forehead in two gold waves, which she twisted up roughly in the back. Her taste led her to wear light colours, and she often pinned a sprig of red fuchsia on her calico waist.

Provided he could see her or only hear her near him, Le Bolloche found nothing to find fault with in life. As Désirée did not stop twisting straw when talking, they chattered while they worked; as she was already at the age which dreams, they talked almost always of the future.

It was at this time precisely that the ordeal began for Père Le Bolloche. First, the wound of his leg, which had never entirely healed, became inflamed. There was no use swearing; gangrene set in, and after weeks of suffering the leg had to be amputated. The whole reserve fund of the household was spent in surgeon's fees, in little vials which were lined up on the mantel, empty, with their red labels. The sick man did not grow more patient lying in bed and seeing his money melt away. There was an entire season of convalescence, and when he resumed his place in the shed he very soon realised that he had lost much more of his body than he had thought. Alas! sickness had consumed the suppleness and the energy, the valour of the muscles which in short is the good humour of our limbs.

Désirée was there, certainly, each day more capable of earning the bread for the household. Thanks to the activity of his daughter and to a slight advance in price, Le Bolloche hoped that the three women, the donkey, hens, and cat, which made up the personnel confided to his care, would not feel too severely the results of this accident, which from a mere wounded man had made of him an invalid. He might earn less, perhaps, but his daughter would earn a little more, and the result would be the same. He was deceived. A second obstacle and an invincible one arose. Neither father nor daughter refused work; it was the work which began to fail. From one season to another the diminution of the orders became more sensible. At first there were hours without work, then entire days. In vain Le Bolloche, with his donkey and cart, continued to scour the suburban quarters and call up to the windows, where fan-shaped ivy geraniums and pyramids of pinks bloomed, his traditional cry: "Chairs to mend; chairs to mend!" Less and less frequently did his cry find an echo. What was the reason? Progress, the invasion of luxury which, from place to place, from château to bourgeois house, and even to farmhouse, supplants old tradition and introduces, in the place of massive framed chairs with rush-covered seats, the light and cheap furniture made in the factories of Paris or Vienna. The triumph of rattan, of upholstered chairs, of woven reed, of white willow rockers by which chair-menders were slowly evicted. A trade was dying! How many others have disappeared in the same way! How many humble workmen, with a desperate astonishment, have felt the tool slipping from their hands and the trade learned in childhood's days, the trade which had honourably supported their father and had sufficed for them for the half of their life, become thus progressively hazardous and unproductive! Is there anything so cruel? Some, without doubt, can seek another trade. But the old, for whom the time of apprenticeship is passed, nailed to these ruined trades, have now only to disappear with them! Such was the case with Père Le Bolloche. The worthy man realised it fully. He let things go with that reservation of hope which we have as long as things still go. Grass began to invade the workshop under the bundles of yellow rye which were rotting under foot. The rushes and reeds in the marsh, formerly cut to the ground, now grew large, swelled and mounted in tufts. And as the majority of our sorrows here below have a reverse side of joy for some one, the song-birds of the quarter did not complain, never having, no, nor those before them, found so much down on the edge of the pond for their young. He waited until the end, until the last cent of their savings was spent. And behold, that hour had arrived! The grandmother, who kept the accounts in her memory, of course, and guarded the purse, had warned her son that very morning. A resolution must be taken, an expedient found, for the next day's bread was no longer assured. That was what Le Bolloche, his long face lengthened still more by sadness, was thinking of this spring day, seated at a little distance from the shed.

To delude his passion for smoking he drew two or three puffs of air through the empty bowl of his pipe, and the first idea which came to him was that he might do without tobacco; he felt that he was capable of this sacrifice. But it did not take him long to perceive that this was not a solution. Then what was to be done? Place Désirée out at service? He would never consent to that; rather, he would beg his bread. Say to the old mother: "We are not able to keep you longer. Seek a home; ask for public charity . . ."? Away with the thought! Could a child even think of it? Sell the house? It would be necessary to rent another, and rents had doubled, tripled, since Le Bolloche had lived in his meadow corner. Where would be the advantage? Plainly, there was but one solution, that of which his wife and he had already spoken. They would both go away; they would leave the house to the grandmother, who was too old, and to Désirée, who was too young and too much loved, to bear such a grief.

Go away! When he had reached this conclusion, Le Bolloche leaned his elbow on his good leg and looked slowly around him, with that glance freighted with farewells which always discovers some new beauty in the most familiar things. The meadow, where the grass was springing up, where the buttercups, escaped from the donkey, were beginning to open, appeared to promise him an abundant hay harvest. The hedges, which on three sides ran around it, no longer had a puny and withered air and those lamentable holes which they once showed. Well supplied with full-fledged thorns, supported with iron wire in the weak places, they defended the house better than a wall. And the wall, which went along the road, although a little moss-grown, was still solid and upright. Le Bolloche had often dreamed of building a house there for his son-in-law, a house like the other which was on the half slope. Ah! if trade had not betrayed him! What a pretty view they would have had, from the windows, of the street which, lighted with gas, leads up to the *octroi*, so gay on a Sunday, so coquettish with its wine-shops, painted in bright colours, its games of bowls, its yoke-elms, and its great gardens all pink with peach-trees in bloom!

At this moment Désirée appeared at the top of the meadow, returning from the town. The wind had tossed her hair about; she was walking, one hand hanging down, the other passed through the broken seat of a chair, which, hung from her arm, surrounded her with an uneven disk of yellow rays. The young girl had walked two miles to find this work. She came back uncomplaining, happy even, in the light of the setting sun which trailed over the meadow. When Le Bolloche saw her he understood better still that separation from her would be the hardest thing of all, that in comparison with that the others were nothing.

"Well!" she said with her good-humoured tone, "you were asking for work; here is some! A chair such as you like to new-bottom in coarse rush."

"No, little one," the good man answered sadly. "I have just finished my last chair and I am sitting on it."

She drew near without comprehending what he was saying, astonished simply that he should be so gloomy. He was joyous usually when she was joyous. What was the matter with him?

"Call your mother," Le Bolloche added; "I have something to say to her."

She went into the house, and her mother, so tiny under her enormous cap, came out. Le Bolloche led his wife to the edge of the stream which ran along the path. He told her his plan, not roughly at all as he was wont to do when he told her the least thing, but almost softly, much troubled himself and out of his usual temper. Désirée watched them from the distance. She saw them side by side, he stooping down a little, her figure, on the contrary, stiffened and her head uplifted. They were conversing in tones low in spite of the calm of the evening, and nothing but the alternate buzzing of their voices and the regular grinding of the leather sheath in which his amputated leg was encased was heard.

When they went into the house, Le Bolloche seated himself in front of the grandmother, sunk down in her armchair provided with pillows, on the right of the chimney-place, and he lifted his hand to his forehead, to salute her with the familiar movement of the old soldier.

"Mother," he said, "the work does not prosper any more."

"That is true, my son!"

"I still eat much for my age," continued Le Bolloche, "more than I earn. This state of things cannot last. I must go away with Victorine."

The old woman of ninety, heavy as she was, began to tremble. With an instinctive movement she tried to open her dead eyes, which now made only a slender slit in the wrinkled recess of the orbit.

"Go away!" she exclaimed, "and where would you go, Honoré?"

Le Bolloche turned half-way around, as if the grandmother were really looking at him and he could not endure her glance. He answered with some confusion:

"To the Little Sisters of the Poor; Victorine claims that one is well taken care of there."

The old woman pulled herself up by the arm of her chair.

"I am the one who will go!" she said with that same harsh tone which she had transmitted to her son.

"No, mother, no! You are too used to this place. We are younger, we two, sorrow will not kill us!"

"But, my child, nothing belongs to me here. I am in——"

"Your own house," said Le Bolloche quickly. And this man, who was himself old and infirm, had the inspiration of a child to convince his mother. He encircled her with his arms and whispered in her ear with a playfulness half feigned, half real:

"Mamma, when I was with the regiment and when I went through the hundred battles, I spent more than my pay, didn't I?"

"Yes."

"Hundreds of sous, ten francs a week. Who paid for it?"

"I did."

"Have I paid you the money back?"

"No."

"Then you see clearly that you are in your own house, since I owe you that!"

She remained a moment without saying anything, then answered:

"Yes, I am willing, only you must take with you some clothes and some furniture so as not to arrive there like a beggar."

"Provided that you have enough left," said Le Bolloche; "I do not ask for anything better."

The grandmother did not say anything more. It was ended. Among the poor, effusive thanks are unknown. There were none in this case. The grandmother, who held her hands clasped across her bosom, raised them twice only to show how deeply she was touched. That was all.

They seated themselves for supper around a salad, which the meadow had furnished them. Saddened by the thought of a change, so great and so near, they did not speak. What was the use? The same regret weighed on them all. They had struggled to the end. Poverty was the strongest. What was the use?

However, Le Bolloche noticed that the grandmother ate nothing. She moved her lips, as if she dared not ask a question which troubled her. Several times, the words stopped thus upon her lips. At last, she made an effort to control herself, and with a voice full of anguish, asked:

"Honoré, are you going to leave me Désirée?"
Two deep sighs answered her, yes.

Then one could have seen the countenance of the aged woman, unexpressive and relaxed like all faces to whom impressions no longer arrive through the eyes, light up with a sudden light. Joy broke the darkness of this blind face. It seemed as if the soul drew near and smiled through it. At the same time, the old couple looked at Désirée with the same dejected look. The place which the young girl held in their hearts was shown thus, without speech, more eloquently than by words. For a child can be shared. One is enough for several old people. And when these poor people had come to live under the same roof, mother, son and daughter-in-law, it was not only their small patrimony, which they had put in common, nor the courage which goes from one to the other of those who work together, nor the mutual aid which their poverty lends, it was more, it was most of all the youth of Désirée.

The supper over, Le Bolloche shook himself a little to chase away this sadness unworthy of a man. While his wife helped the grandmother to bed, he drew Désirée outside and, in the warmth of the night already come, began walking with her from the shed, which ended the house on the right, to the hutch in the latticework nailed to the wall on the left.

Perceiving that her eyes were red, he said:

"Come, come, Désirée, that will pass! Courage! Look at me. I do not cry, and yet I am sorry to leave you, believe me, especially to leave you unmarried!"

"Why so?"

"Because it was my wish to see you established. We would have chosen your husband together, an old soldier like myself. While down there, you understand——"

He did not finish his thought, and, crossing his arms, he stood still, fixing his eyes in the eyes of his daughter:

"At least, tell me, before I go, a thing which I would like to know."

In her turn, she looked at him with her frank glance in which there shone the brightness of the stars.

"Have you a sweetheart?"

The question struck Désirée as droll; she replied, laughing in spite of her sadness:

"Why, no, father, I have no one."

"It is true, you hardly ever go anywhere, and they never see you. If those who are of the age to seek a wife had seen you! Well, Désirée, if you are of my blood, as I believe, you will never marry any one but a retired soldier."

"A retired soldier?"

"Oh! he may be retired without being old! Provided that he has carried arms and made a campaign, that will be enough for me, I shall be satisfied. Every soldier is not decorated as I am."

"Surely."

"About the regiment, I leave you the choice. A zouave, naturally, would suit me best, but you can also marry a cavalryman. There are some fine little dragoons."

"Well, then," replied the young girl, "a zouave or a dragoon."

"Even a rifleman, that is a choice corps," resumed Le Bolloche, "but not an infantryman, you understand?"

"No."

"Above all not a civilian! What would I find to talk about with him, when I saw him? Remember that, Désirée, if you bring me a 'Blue,' a man who has never seen service, I refuse!"

He became quite pompous in saying that, one arm extended toward the town. This old non-commissioned officer had never been able to get rid of a certain leaning to melodrama. The pompousness of his speech meant nothing, however; Désirée knew that. She was about to answer "no," doubtless to please him, but Le Bolloche, letting his eyes follow the direction of his uplifted arm, saw the slate roofs, one above the other shining under the moonlight like silver shells; the rising line of street lamps which, in the blue immensity of the night, look like miserable yellow points—the whole quarter, which he had so often traversed for so many years. How many tranquil people he knew, behind those lighted windows, certain of sleeping to-morrow in the same room, where they were still awake this evening! The thought hurt him; he turned abruptly away saying:

"Let us go in, Désirée, the dew is falling."

II.

The next day, on the road leading to the Little Sisters of the Poor, to *Jeanne Jugan*, as they called it in the faubourg, a donkey dragged the strangest load which had ever weighed upon his pack-saddle of poverty. In the first place, upon the seat of the low cart, Le Bolloche in a brown frock coat, his zouave cap on his head, and by his side his wife in her best dress of checked fustian, her eyes wet with tears behind her horn spectacles; then, exactly upon the line of the axle, a pyramid, made up of a box in which their everyday clothes were placed; a second box, pierced with holes, which contained a family of rabbits, accustomed to the dim light; and crowning all a basket, from which emerged, in white and black tufts, the feathers of a couple of Barbary fowls, who were kept in the basket by rods; lastly, three pots of sweet basil, one large one flanked by two smaller ones of luxuriant, rounded, superb growth, lashed by a cord to the floor of the vehicle, ended the load in the back. There was besides, between the two good people, a small, thin grey cat, the companion of the chair-mender, who occasionally rubbed her head like a viper along her master's leg.

They were on their way, people, animals, furniture, to the dwelling where so many similar wrecks had preceded them. It took three-quarters of an hour to reach there on foot and more than an hour at the donkey's gait. But what

mattered that to Le Bolloche? He was in no
hurry to get to the end of that journey. He did
not cry, as formerly, through the streets: "Chairs
to mend; chairs to mend!" He was no longer
anything in the world, not even a weaver of rushes,
and he felt it cruelly. When he raised his eyes
to the houses of his former clients, on one side or
the other, his heartrending smile answered the
astonishment which his turnout provoked. Small
boys standing barefoot on thresholds laughed; tall
girls appeared at the windows and with a shrug
of the shoulders, still holding in their arms the
straw mattresses which they were beating, leaned
out to catch a glimpse at what was passing below.
This move excited their mirth. They did not
suspect the sorrow of these two travellers. Still
the woman, more gentle by nature, had become
a little resigned, but the man felt a violent grief
in which much wounded pride was mingled. The
idea of shutting himself up, a man who had commanded a section, under the authority of a woman,
especially of a nun, irritated him to the highest
degree. He had a spite in advance against the one
who was going to receive him. And as he neared
the end of his journey his face became more stern,
his eyebrows knit together, he had his grand air
of the days of a review. Le Bolloche meant to
impose it on them from the first. They should
not take him for a drone at the end of his resources,
tired of roaming about and begging shelter; certainly not, nor for a man without character, who
can be ordered about like a child. The first nun
to see him would not make a mistake!

Finally the road began to ascend. A white mill rose on the right, and the mill adjoined the hospital; with a strip of meadow separating them, they occupied the entire top of the hill. The travellers stopped for a moment. In front, at the end of the road, two very high buildings projected at an open angle, hiding the rest of the house, which revealed thus only its two outstretched arms. An encircling wall turned and followed the slope on the other side. Above it tops of trees, with new leaves, rose here and there. All the windows were open. Le Bolloche urged the donkey to the foot of a flight of steps and waited.

A hospital is like a beehive: one never waits long without seeing a bee come out. A sister's cap appeared and beneath it a very tiny, very young, and very dark sister.

"What do you want?" she asked.

"To see the one in command here." replied Le Bolloche austerely.

"Is it to sell anything to her? The good mother is very busy, you see; and if it is for that——"

"Have I the air of a travelling merchant?" replied Le Bolloche. "You do not understand at all, Mademoiselle." He insisted on the word, knowing very well that he emancipated himself from a respectful tradition. "I wish to speak with her, to make a business proposition to her. and a good one, too."

The sister glanced at the travellers, the box, the three pots of sweet basil.

"I understand," she said, "my worthy man;

I will go in and fetch her." And she turned away so swiftly that he could not tell whether she had disappeared behind the pillar of the right or that to the left.

"Worthy man, indeed!" he grumbled; "there's a silly jade for you, to call me 'worthy man'!"

He slipped down the length of the step and stood erect, the reins of cord wrapped around his arm, the saucy zouave cap perched on the back of his head, a little to one side.

A shadow flitted by the arched window of the cloister and a second sister appeared on the threshold of the door; she was of average height, but so frail that she appeared small. Her hands, which she held clasped on her black gown, were white and transparent. It would have been difficult to have told her age. All the features of her delicate face were made still thinner by fatigue and the consuming struggle of an ardent soul. There was not, however, a wrinkle to be seen. There was something infantine in her glance, and at the same time she had the compassionate smile of a person who has lived. Her cap concealed the colour of her hair. She was the "good mother," a great lady, who governed two hundred poor people and sixty nuns with a move of her fingers.

She looked at the equipage standing in front of her for a moment. The corners of her thin lips curled up involuntarily, by a surprise of her nature, which was gay and sprightly in the world. But her will immediately repressed this unruly movement, and she said with her voice, which had neither tone nor song, but was very soft nevertheless:

"You have come to enter with us?"

Le Bolloche, somewhat disconcerted, answered: "Yes, Madame, if you have room."

"We will make room, my friend, and we will serve you to the best of our ability."

"Moreover, I do not ask for charity; I bring my household things."

"And even your cat!"

"All that is yours," he continued, including in a sweeping motion the donkey, wagon, and load. "I place only two conditions."

"What are they?"

"Just now, one of your inferiors——"

"You mean to say one of our sisters?"

"Yes; I am an old soldier, you see; all that is not superior is inferior. Well, then, your sister called me 'worthy man.' I do not like that."

"You must pardon us if we do it again," said the sister, upon whose face the same light smile reappeared; "it is a sort of habit with us."

"And then I would like to know whether one has the liberty of his belief here? I prefer to tell you at once, I do not believe much, I am not devout. I am not a hypocrite. And if one has not the liberty of his opinions here, I do not stay!"

Le Bolloche said this with his grandest air. He saw with astonishment that the sister smiled openly, with a smile so beaming, so deep, so fresh that he lost countenance.

"Well!" he exclaimed, "since it is my opinion——"

"Fear nothing," she replied; "we have several worthy men here who think as you do."

Then she came down the steps and gave her

hand to help Mère Le Bolloche, who was quite frightened by the boldness of her husband, get down from the wagon.

He had already begun to unharness the donkey.

"Lead him to the stable," said the sister, "yonder; yes, that is it—turn to the left—straight ahead before you now."

On all sides of Le Bolloche numerous service buildings, stable, pig-pen, hen-house, cow-shed, were extended, and upon the slope of the hill on the side opposite the entrance lay a large field of rye, with borders of dwarf apple-trees.

A whole population of slow, bent, broken, stumbling old men were walking about in the paths. There were as many crutches as sound legs. The sullen wind which, above, was chasing the greyish-brown clouds would have been able, without difficulty, to topple these poor human ruins to the ground. Looking at them, Le Bolloche began pitying his own fate. He unharnessed the donkey and fastened it to a manger which he filled with hay.

"You, at least," said he, "will not suffer."

Afterward he set himself to the task of unloading the wagon, and, beginning with the basket, he lifted up the rods which held captive the cock and hen. As soon as he was out the cock flapped his wings and began crowing. The hen scratched her beak among the tufts of grass in the court and pecked without the least perturbation. Old Le Bolloche, who was inclined at this moment to make sad comparisons, shrugged his shoulders.

"Animals," he murmured, "do not see any difference; here or there, it is all the same to them!" And with the back of his sleeve he wiped away a tear which no one, happily, had seen falling.

III.

These pensioners of Jeanne Jugan were indeed ruins, ruins of all kinds and all origins. Some had been poor all their life, others had fallen from a small competency or even from a fortune. The causes which had brought them there, in this refuge where charity blinded its eyes to receive them, varied little; it was misfortune for some, misconduct for many. Certain ones had worn out twenty professions, run all over Europe and America, taken photographs for Paris shopkeepers, gathered snails for restaurants, picked moss for florists in the woods of Viroflay, and lassoed wild animals on the prairies of La Plata; they had tried their hand at everything, had taken root nowhere, and, driven by hunger, had gone to the Little Sisters with the secret hope of leaving there again.

They all lived a common life, but not in the same way. Discoveries of like tastes and origin, similarities of trade or even of suffering, grouped them into little companies for walk or work. For they worked at the hospital; oh! as a play, children's work, which, deserted at their whim, did not last long and brought in nothing. A few weavers plied the loom for an hour or two in a low room; half a dozen tailors sewed the rents in coats that had been already mended; the farmers took care of the horse and cows, cut grass, or braided baskets; the hay-making in fine weather brought the strongest together for a fortnight in the small meadow; from one end of the year to the other, those able to hold a spade dug up a bit of ground or cut the weeds in a small garden which was assigned to them as their own and of which they parcelled out the cultivation as they pleased, one into a kitchen garden, another into a tiny orchard, another into a flower-plot. There were also the incorrigible drones or the feeble who did nothing. Charity watched over them and for them, laboured and smiled; she took no rest that they might enjoy complete repose. She could have been called rich, she found so many ways to be amiable and helpful. Her patience had no limit. She practised the thankless art of being motherly to the old.

Le Bolloche quickly had his group of followers. They were all the old soldiers, scattered until then and floating about in the population of the hospital. The eloquence of the old non-commissioned officer, his imposing bearing, the magic brightness of the corporal's and sergeant's chevrons which they imagined they saw in rays of gold on his pensioner's sleeve, attracted them. They listened to him willingly. In their midst Le Bolloche had again the illusion of the barracks and of command. A most mixed battalion without doubt, where all branches of the service were mingled and of which several officers came from disciplinary companies. But what mattered it? They belonged to the profession. They put their campaigns together. Each told his story, often the same one, but never in the same way. They had a way of their own of talking of war. Each had seen but a small corner of the field of battle. Many of them had remained under arms half a day exposed to the rain of bursting shells. Their accounts gave a poor and mutilated idea of military things. They delighted in them, however, and continually returned to them apropos of some detail which they did not remember to have told.

On days of going out those who returned from town with a paper read marvellous news to the others. They grew heated over the prodigious armaments of Russia or Germany, the guns capable of piercing trunks of oak-trees, fifty inches through, the smokeless powder, the submarine boats, the trials of torpedoes. The most ultra-patriotic gave the tone, the old renewed their youth, a ferment of ancient, glorious fevers ran through their veins. Then, what defiances against all hostile peoples, what oaths of love for their France, what predictions of victory! They all saw the victorious army crossing the frontier and falling upon the villages of the Rhine. They imagined themselves a part of it, they pillaged, they killed, they became intoxicated and fell asleep in the little white sheets of the conquered. At such times Le Bolloche was superb. He commanded them all, with his voice still resonant with the alcohol of the canteen. Steps were hastened, canes uplifted, rheumatic arms stretched out in front. Poor old men! Their French troopers' hearts had not grown old.

They talked of these exciting questions usually in the rye-field, where the ears were beginning to appear. When a sister passed on the terrace of the hospital above, she stopped for a moment, astonished at such great animation. She followed these warriors with a tranquil eye, always counting them, fearful that the count was not exact "There are our little old men, who are talking of war," she thought. The kind of pleasure which they took in it was completely foreign to her, but she was not sorry to see them so martial. It gave her the feeling which boys playing noisily with leaden soldiers give to their mothers. Then, satisfied with her inspection, the white cap went away. The little old men had not seen her.

The rule was not severe. Le Bolloche acknowledged even that it did not displease him. He had the illusion of activity and the reality of repose. His comrades gave full satisfaction to his taste for praise. He had a good appetite, suffered little from his leg, breathed the air of the hills for eight hours a day, to which the near course of a great river, stretched and ramified to infinity in the green country, like the blue veins of a thistle-leaf, gave life. But for all that he pined visibly away; the hollow wrinkles of his cheeks sunk deeper still. He had periods of dumbness and moroseness, which the sisters did not mistake. Sister Dorothée tried a supplementary ration of tobacco, usually a most efficacious remedy. Le Bolloche accepted it, thanked her, and smoked it; but he was not cheered up.

"Perhaps he would like to see his wife oftener?" the sister thought, and, in place of twice a week, Le Bolloche was allowed to meet daily, in a corridor of the hospital, his wife, who was quite at home and very gentle and retiring there as elsewhere. They talked a little; but they had not much to say to each other, never having had the same turn of mind and having no longer the same life. The good man did not return from these visits of favour any more gay.

By dint of thinking about it, Sister Dorothée had an inspiration.

Observing him standing motionless in the middle of the garden, his foot on his spade, looking fixedly toward the lower part of the town, the veiled horizons where houses, streets, and gardens have no longer a distinct shape and become but shadows in the softened scale of distances, she guessed his thought:

"It is your daughter that you miss?" she said.

Le Bolloche, who had not seen the sister, trembled at this word. His old face became hard, his eyes kindled with a sombre fire; he did not like to have any one know his affairs, and the discovery of a grief, which he was too proud to confide to any one, wounded him as an indiscretion.

But soon the emotion that the words "your daughter" caused him was the strongest. He could not master it, it carried him away entirely, it changed him. His features relaxed and, humbly, softly, in a tone through which the confession of his long suffering pierced, he replied:

"It is true!"

"Why did you not say so sooner?" continued the sister. "You have not seen her during the five weeks that you have been here?"

"No."

"Would you like me to write to her to come?"

"Oh! yes!"

"You love this Désirée so much?"

He had not the strength to reply. His hands trembled on the handle of his shovel, and his eyes, which he turned away, saw doubtless in imagination standing in the grass of the meadow the child who came to him.

That evening when Sister Dorothée asked permission of the superior to write, she added:

"This little old man is incredible; you would say that he was the mother!"

And covering a sheet of paper with an irregular and hurried handwriting, she posted it to the address of Désirée.

IV.

If the young girl had not yet visited her parents, it had not been for want of thinking of it. But her grandmother had fallen quite seriously ill, and she was, like many persons when they are ill, extremely exacting. Solitude inspired her with horror. It had been necessary to nurse her, watch her, and never leave her. She barely gave Désirée time to go to the edge of the village for supplies. How would she have permitted a visit to the hospital, which, considering the long distance, would have taken a whole morning? Désirée had to wait and the weeks had slipped by.

Sister Dorothée's letter came when the invalid was in full convalescence, and these two causes combined, the entreaties on one side, the reviving health on the other, decided the grandmother.

"Go, my child," she said. "Be as quick as possible. You will bring me news of Honoré."

She hardly thought of her daughter-in-law, any more in the present than she had in the past. Honoré alone filled her thoughts.

Désirée started at once. She was happy in the thought of seeing her parents again, happy also to be free and in the beauty of the day. The sky was covered with fleecy grey clouds through which all the rays pierced, one of those skies of the end of May, which accustom the flowers to the intense sun of summer. Starflowers dotted the slopes of the suburbs. The sparrows, perched on the roofs and the old walls on both sides of the road, flew away in flocks, when Désirée passed, with a little cry of appeal, so gay and so quick that it seemed to Désirée that her heart was flying away too. It did not fly very far, however, no more than they. Hers was not a dreamy nature, but rather an active and a courageous one. She thought about the orders that must be delivered during the week, of some washing that she would soon have, of a sowing of convolvulus which she had made along the house and which was beginning to sprout, but most of all of a way to braid rattan and willow now that her childhood's trade was dying out. She had put on her blue dress, a white collar fastened by a cornelian brooch and a hat—for so long a journey—composed of a single blue ribbon crumpled upon some black tulle. It was the finest thing she had. Any one else would have thought her toilet very poor. But about that she cared little; her only care, for the moment, was that of pleasing those whom she was going to see. She was sure of succeeding there. And thus dressed, thinking of the ever-complicated problem of her life of work, trying to solve it, she walked without haste, along the road, where silly breezes, blowing through the hedges, amused themselves by whirling up pinches of dust.

Before entering the hospital Désirée, a little tired, a little red, stopped in front of the mill to get her breath and to knot up her hair, whose too heavy mass, loosened by her walk, fell upon her neck. The road stopped a few paces from there. A knoll on the grass, trampled by the feet of mules, bore the white mill. Its four great wings turned with a powerful movement, with a soft creaking of bending wood, such as comes from the masts of ships, or from the yokes of oxen in ploughing. The wind swept up from the river. Désirée, with her head bare, her figure bent back, her arms upstretched twisting her golden hair, was charming.

That is precisely what a young miller was thinking who, without her seeing him, was leaning on his elbows out of the garret window of the mill.

Millers have, in all ages, been considered philosophers and contemplative persons. I speak of those who live on heights. Their trade makes them so. They combine the nature of the hermit and the lighthouse-keeper. One part of their life is spent in waiting, the other in letting the wind do their work. They see vast horizons and also the little things beneath them. When their nature is not averse to it, millers have a fine opportunity for dreaming.

This one was not inconsistent with tradition. His wide felt hat, white with flour, covered a rather fine head; he was a young man, a little indolent but intelligent, with brown eyes, colourless cheeks, and a mouth slightly raised at the corners, giving to his face a good-natured teasing air, a distinctive sign of the class. He leaned a little farther out of the window and said:

"You don't appear to be hurried, Mademoiselle?"

Such are the commonplace phrases with which, among the people, persons who are not acquainted try each other and show their willingness to engage in a bit of conversation. Surprised, she looked up at him, and not finding his look too bold, answered:

"Nor you, either, from what I see."

"What is there to do?" he resumed; "when the mill is going, millers have nothing better to do than to look at the passing girls. It is a fine trade; even when work goes best, one has some freedom."

"All trades are not the same," said Désirée, sighing.

She knotted the faded strings of her hat and

turned to go. But evidently she pleased him, for he detained her, saying:

"What do you do, then?"

"I am a chair-mender," she answered. "The trade was good once and we earned our living. Then it died away. My father was obliged to go to the hospital. He was a good workman, however, I assure you; never behindhand and not a spendthrift. Everybody liked him."

"He is at Jeanne Jugan?"

"Yes, and so is my mother; I am going to see them."

"Then you are like an orphan at home, Mademoiselle Rose?"

"No, not Rose," she said, laughing; "Désirée."

They looked at each other a moment, both laughing at the droll manner in which he had asked her name. She added:

"I am not so alone as you think; my grandmother is with me."

"Do you live far from here?"

"On the other side of the town, near the *octroi*. My grandmother is blind."

"Blind!" repeated the young man; "that cannot be very gay for you."

"It is especially sad for her."

"Then you go out but little."

"Scarcely at all."

"On a Sunday, don't you? A turn at the fair, or perhaps in the assemblies?"

"Never!" exclaimed Désirée, as if that supposition had offended her. "I never go there."

She began blushing, becoming suddenly confused at the intimate turn which the conversation was taking. He, on the contrary, showed his white teeth. He looked perfectly satisfied.

"I believe you, Mademoiselle Désirée; one can see that without your saying so. Au revoir then!"

"Good evening, Monsieur."

Scarcely had she turned the corner of the hedge before she felt vexed with herself. To stop thus to talk on the road! How came she to do such a thing? And how many things she had talked about in a short time! About her father, her mother, her grandmother, the life they led at home. He had made her tell all that he wished, and he prudently knew how to keep silent. How cunning he was, that fellow, in wheedling girls! Before entering the court, as she was hidden by the wall, she turned her head quickly and cast a glance in the direction of the mill. The garret window was empty, all black on the white wall. "Happily," Désirée thought, "he had an honest look and no one saw me."

She went up the flight of steps and asked for her father.

Le Bolloche was outside in the centre of an open and sandy place which lay at the foot of the field of rye. They had chosen him for umpire of a doubtful play at bowls, and, bent over, he was measuring the disputed distance with his cane. Half a score of players, his comrades, stooping in a circle, were absorbed by the interest of this verification. They all rose up together, and Le Bolloche saw Désirée, who was walking along the field, her blue frock grazing the dwarf apple-trees and the border of strawberry-plants blooming freely beneath.

"My daughter!" he exclaimed.

It was an event, the arrival of those twenty years in an asylum of old men, that radiant health in the midst of all those human infirmities. The comrades of Le Bolloche, ball in hand, looked at the young girl coming. Almost all without family, having roved everywhere, without taking root anywhere, isolated besides by their age and already shut up in that semi-death of the refuge, which charity can never completely disguise, they took in, like a perfume, this apparition which was advancing. All were gladdened by it. To each one she recalled some pleasant memory.

"She looks like a pretty canteen girl I used to know," said one.

"If she wore her hair on her forehead, would not one swear that she was an actress of the café of the Dajo promenade?" said another, an old sailor, whose memory flowed very far back at the sight of Désirée. A third murmured a name, which no one heard. His head, twitching with spasmodic jerks, dropped on his chest and two tears fell upon the woollen rags with which his sore feet were wrapped, and no one knew what distant image of a woman or of a young girl, the emotion of this forsaken one was saluting through the past years.

They watched Le Bolloche go to meet Désirée, pass his arm in hers and disappear in the path which cut the fields half-way. Roused from their rapture, they looked at each other then with a hard air. They were jealous of the former sergeant. No one came thus for them. The game of bowls was abandoned. Le Bolloche and his daughter both walked at first in the path. He was radiant, his happiness doubled by the pride of walking by her side. He enjoyed the astonishment which she aroused. He looked at her as if to accustom his eyes to each of the features of his child.

"Ah, little one!" he cried. "Little one, how happy I am! I cannot live without seeing you!" He could not utter a word more.

Then Mère Le Bolloche came to find them. They walked up toward the hospital of which it was necessary to make the tour to the large orchard surrounded by walls and only opened by favour to visiting relatives. And then the talk began.

Désirée had to place herself between the two old people, talking to her at the same time, each of what interested them. The most unimportant things came to life again in their memory with a marvellous intensity of tenderness and of regret. It is incredible how many questions a meadow, a house, and a poor grandmother whom one has left can furnish. Désirée replied as best she could; their joy made her expansive too. She had no time to think of herself. And yet, every time that she came to the turn of a certain path, the shadow of the wings of the mill leaping the walls ran before her, enveloped her, seemed to wish to carry her away in passing. Désirée felt a little thrill; she imagined very wrongfully, per-

haps, and without having the right to think of it
so, that these great shadowy arms beckoned to
her and that there were two brown eyes down
there which were following her through an unknown crevice of the mill.

V.

When Désirée returned home, she found the
old grandmother less anxious than she had expected. Happy to tell her:

"Little one, there came a fine order during
your absence; twelve chairs to be new-bottomed
in black and white! One would say that business
is going to look up again."

Désirée had no illusions on this subject, but the
work was none the less welcome. The very next
day, wholly rested and refreshed by the afternoon
of the day before, she set herself to work. She had
to carry out of the shed the sheaves of sorted rye,
which a too long stay in the shade had rendered
damp, to loosen them and spread them out in
regular rows on a mowed corner of the meadow.
And while the sun and air were drying them she
busied herself removing the worn seats from the
chairs, with strengthening their bars and staining some handfuls of stalks, which would make
regular spots upon the new seats, like ermine
tails upon white fur. All that occupied two days.

During this time she thought, indeed several
times, of the meeting which she had had with the
miller, without displeasure, but without emotion,
either; just as we think of things which will have

no continuation. In going to buy her supplies in the quarter of the *octroi*, she looked for the wings of the mill on the horizon, and she saw them turning, very tiny, like a child's toy.

The third day, in the evening, seeing that the straw was dry and that it had regained its beautiful pale-gold tint, she thought that it was time to gather it together again. In slender sheaves and carefully, in order not to crush the straight stalks of rye, she picked it up and carried it under the shed. One would have thought her a harvester. She loved to handle this supple and quivering straw, which every step made tremble under her arm; it pleased her to run thus the length of the meadow, through the grass which was still warm from the scorching rays of the sun it had absorbed.

The least thing which took her out of doors seemed a diversion to this industrious girl. At the moment when she was picking up the last armfuls of straw, the sun had long since set, and twilight was invading the faubourg. And just then, in straightening up, Désirée saw the shape of a man's head above the wall, which was painted like a brown ribbon along the west. She was not at a loss for a moment; it was he! A blush mounted to her face. She bent quickly down, seized the rest of her straw, and, without turning toward the gate, re-entered the shed.

When she came out the young man, or the form that she had taken for him, had vanished. What had he come for? How long a time had he been looking at her? Oh! this was a serious thing! Why was he, who had called her the first day from the window of his mill, afraid of her now? For he had disappeared as soon as she had looked at him. Disappeared? Perhaps he had hidden himself. All these questions followed in rapid succession in the mind of Désirée.

"After all," she said to herself, "that boy cannot wish me any harm. I would like to know what has become of him, and I will go and see."

She went up the meadow in the tall grass, walked along the wall, and bravely, at the spot where the apparition had vanished, placing her foot upon a projecting stone, she raised herself up so that half her body was above the wall. The road fled flaky and grey. No one was in sight but a peasant, who was trotting down the slope in his covered cart. Yet she had not been mistaken. She examined the top of the wall—the sprigs of moss which covered it, and the starry branches of a yellow plant blossoming there, were crushed at that spot; some one had been leaning there. She looked farther along, and, upon a naked piece of slate, torn from the wall, she recognised vaguely by the last ray of daylight that some letters had been traced. She picked up the stone, turned it toward the west which a last fringe of pale gold lighted up, and read: "Désirée." Who else could have written that name there? The dew of a single night would have sufficed to efface the characters traced by the point of the knife, while, on the contrary, upon the edge of each stroke, a down of dust raised by the cut still remained. It was he then who, a little before, had looked at her, when she picked up the sheaves of rye, and, to make her understand what he dared not say to her, to show her that he thought of her, had written: "Désirée." In short, this word was a letter.

A love-letter! What does "Désirée" signify, if not "I love you"?

He loved her then? The young girl took up the piece of slate and went into the house. Her grandmother was waiting.

"You have been a long time," she said; "the angelus has rung in two parishes!"

Désirée read for the tenth time, by the light of a candle, the word written on the stone.

"Were you only anxious to work?" continued the grandmother. "Come, eat a little.—Why don't you answer? Are you tired?"

But she only answered with some careless words, and the grandmother, at the altered sound of her granddaughter's voice, confirmed in the thought that the child was jaded out, said coaxingly:

"You give yourself too much trouble, my poor child, you stay too late in the shed, and that changes your voice."

Désirée declared that she was tired, exhausted; and the grandmother pretended to be sleepy earlier than usual on that evening.

Then, free to think, to reflect on what had happened, and on what she experienced herself, the young girl gave herself up to imagination. She was then loved! That seemed to her very certain and very sweet. Suspicion did not once suggest to her that he had meant to joke. The first uncertain and veiled word of love, the first homage paid to her charm as a young girl, had touched the depths of this primitive nature. She responded to it at once by great heart-throbs which surprised her. And, little by little, she realised that these thoughts which filled her now were born the very day when she had met this youth. A deep and delicious agitation succeeded. To-morrow, the future, to be married, to be happy! She was agitated by these magic and vague pictures, as tiny streams, with shadowy banks, which feel to their very source the call of the invisible sea. All the details of their brief interview revived. She recalled the questions which he had asked, the slightest words that he had spoken, so as to discover in them also a new meaning. She succeeded but too well.

One thing which Désirée had not noticed at first began to trouble her. She had said that she never went to assemblies.

"I believe you," he had said, smiling. "One can see that without your saying so."

How then had he guessed it? No doubt, he thought her too poor and too meanly dressed. Girls who go for a walk on Sunday, those who can pretend to be pleasing, are differently dressed. He had warned her of that.

"One can see plainly that you have not pretty ways and that you do not know how to dress yourself."

Yes, that was what the phrase and the accompanying smile meant. If he should see her again thus, when she returned to see her father and passed near the white mill, the passing fancy which she had been able to inspire would disappear. Désirée le Bolloche was not well enough dressed, not attractive enough, for a man to be proud of walking with her on his arm. Above all this, for he must be rich, he must like pretty dresses, gloves, and hats with feathers, and the small reddish-brown shoes which the work-girls of the town and even the young dairy-maids from the country wore. While she! Ah, bitter poverty! Ah, the happiness of those who have a little money with which to make themselves beautiful!

Soon this sad reflection chased away all the others. The love-song, barely begun, degenerated into a wail. Désirée remained awake half of the night. Then slowly a plan matured. She hesitated, rejected it, then entertained it again.

She was at work the next day before dawn. She hurried so feverishly that she had never before accomplished so much. In less time than they had allowed her, the twelve chairs were ready to be delivered and paid for. Désirée, when she brought home the money, said to her grandmother:

"Grandmother, if you are willing, I will go to Jeanne Jugan to-morrow."

"To-morrow, child—that is very soon. It is not ten days since you saw them!"

"Grandmother, let me go; I have finished the work."

The grandmother replied after a moment:

"I see plainly that you are no longer happy here, my child. I am too old, and you are too young. I knew that would be the way when your father went away. Go then, as it will give you pleasure!"

Neither spoke again of this absence on the next day.

Désirée tried to be gentle and kind. She helped her grandmother undress, and, on the pretext of some sewing to do, she waited, seated by the table.

When her grandmother was asleep, the young girl dressed, threw a small cape over her shoulders, went cautiously out of the room and, crossing the meadow, was soon on the road which led to the town. She hastened her steps, a little anxious at being alone at this already late hour. Some workmen who passed her looked boldly at her. She felt afraid of the dark hollows of the path. It seemed to her at every moment that some one was following her. And yet the thought never occurred to her to turn back. Her plan gave her courage, and made her smile at times. She walked on. The streets soon became better lighted. The fronts of shops gleamed on the right and the left. She walked more peacefully. The people passing protected her by their number. At last she stopped before the door of a large shop for novelties, which threw the light of its electric lamps at the two corners of the boulevard.

That was the place. With a little hesitation, she went in, dazzled, her eyes half closed. There were but a few customers in the immense shop. A clerk came to her and asked, with that impertinent air which they readily assume when a girl is alone, poor, and pretty:

"What department does Mademoiselle wish to visit? Silks, laces, trousseaux, layettes?"

"What department?" Désirée had never been in a large shop.

"Yes," he repeated, "what do you wish to see?"

Then her secret escaped from her, and she said, not at all as a reply, but speaking to herself in a dreamy tone and as if she saw some far-off, strangely beautiful thing:

"I would like a red parasol!"

She had not far to go. She was shown at first the high-priced parasols, those covered with silk, fringed, and mounted on carved handles. Among the number there were some red ones, but Désirée had not much money. She had to go where the lowest-priced ones were kept. Finally she found what she was looking for—a parasol of ordinary material, white on the outside, lined with a rather bright mauve, which could pass for red. The curved handle was white. Désirée bought it. She also bought a pair of open-worked lisle-thread gloves of simple design, having noticed that even poor girls like herself began to be unwilling to go out on Sundays with their hands bare.

And she began to walk back toward the suburb, along the streets less and less lighted and peopled with passers-by. But she felt no more fear now. She carried the parasol rolled up in a case of grey paper under her arm. She would not have carried a treasure more joyously. It was a treasure to her, since it was to make herself more beautiful, to win better the love of this young miller, that she had spent, without telling her grandmother, a great part of her earnings of the whole week. How fine she would look to-morrow, when at midday she would walk up to Jeanne Jugan, toward the mill which perhaps would have its window open again! She thought of that and the return road seemed short to her.

She entered the house in the darkness. Her grandmother had not awakened. All the crickets of the meadow were singing around the house, under the blades of tall grass.

VI.

The following day, in the afternoon, Désirée went to the hospital. In so short a time, how everything had grown! The dahlias of the courtyard towered a foot above their supports, the climbing roses, open altogether in the June sunshine, overflowed in red and yellow waves the mossy edge of the walls. On seeing that the visitor was his former mistress, the Barbary cock, whose small body enjoyed the right of free passage, came out from the shelter of a spindle-tree, following the young girl as if she had still some small grain in her apron.

Désirée, who was in a good humour, turned toward it and asked:

"Little one, do you know where Père Le Bolloche is?" He answered with such a kirikiki, with so droll and so decided a tone, that she could not help laughing.

"Gone out!" she repeated; "what are you telling me? At least he is in the orchard, is he not, Sister?"

"Really, Mademoiselle, I do not know," answered the nun, who was passing, "I do not know indeed; at this season all our little old men are stirring."

The sun gave new life in truth to the pensioners of Jeanne Jugan. With the exception of certain ones, too faded to freshen up again, who would have recognised them? They raked paths, weeded beds, walked with a gait twice as brisk as that of winter. Several made drawings on the sand with their crutches. There was one gathering cherries, astride of a branch. All wore a light jacket made out of pieces of ticking, by hands which suffered nothing to go to waste.

Day of respite, of illusion which spreads a great sweet light over human sufferings!

Désirée questioned the one gathering cherries.

"Are you asking for the sergeant, my pretty girl?"

"Yes, Père Le Bolloche."

"He is mowing in the meadow."

"What do you say?"

"I say that he is mowing in the meadow. He even commands the squad. You see he is full of vigour and youth, that man!"

And the good man gallantly slipped down to the ground to direct the daughter of Honoré le Bolloche.

"You do not know the way," he said seriously, "and, you see, we do not work by the hour here! One has always time to do the work."

They went up the slope, turned to the right of the hospital and, through a bar which cut the wall of the enclosure, penetrated into a long meadow following the enclosure. This meadow, shaped like a crown and with a growing hedge like a green ring, enclosed the domain of the Sisters and bordered upon the miller's knoll.

When she reached there, Désirée saw a new sight. Eight old men, armed with eight scythes, their shirt-sleeves rolled up, were mowing in a line in the tall grass. Le Bolloche in the middle, the tallest of all, his wooden leg forward, was working like a young man. It was wonderful to see the width of the circular swath which went down before him at each stroke of his scythe. He did not stop as the others did, who, under pretext of sharpening their scythes, whetted a short quarter of an hour on their blade. He was on fatigue duty and took the work seriously. Chief of the squad, imagine it! It was a matter of pride with him to appear indefatigable, to round out his arm to its full extent, and especially not to allow himself to be distracted; no, not even when an old sister passed behind the line of mowers, a jug of cider in her hand, and said:

"Come, my friends, do not work too much; drink a little. It is so warm!"

Désirée approached. He looked at her with a vexed air.

"You can see very well," he said, "that I have some work to do! Go wait for me down yonder. Mowing, my child, is like furbishing: it cannot be interrupted!"

And, as he said that, he was superb, his head upright, his hand leaning upon his lifted scythe; he felt that he was admired by his comrades, ruins more dilapidated than he.

"Down yonder!" he repeated.

Désirée went to the place which the gesture of the good man indicated, a little farther off in the meadow, by the side of the hedge. There she seated herself on the grass, not without noticing that the mill was close by and that it was not turning. The thought of the miller had scarcely left her; it had occupied her all along the way; it made her heart beat more quickly now than usual, under her flowered cotton bodice. And the thought which holds us, you know, poses and shapes us to its fancy. The young girl did not look at the hedge, certainly, but she watched it from the corner of her bright eyes, wandering over the meadow. She expected something which was coming from there. She felt herself very near a serious moment, and a mysterious one too, of her life. She trembled at a breath of air in the brambles. The gliding of a field-mouse over the dead leaves seemed to her a step which was approaching. At times she closed her eyes to recover herself, and not to yield to a kind of vertigo which seized her. She felt a wish to say to the daisies, (a foolish idea which she had never had before!): "Do not look at me so, all together, with your eyes of gold. I am a poor girl whom usually you do not care for!" It seemed to her that these thousands of witnesses were observing her agitated air. She clasped then, with her gloved hand, the parasol which bathed her cheeks, her forehead, all her fair person, with a pink reflection. The idea that her parasol made her prettier, and gave her the look of a young lady, passed through her mind. And, smiling, happy and anxious at the same time, among the daisies which surrounded her with their flowers or sowed the down of their seeds upon her dress, she was more charming still.

The intense midday heat warmed the meadow; the perfume of the hay rose from it like the incense of summer. The mowers advanced, swinging their arms. How long did she remain thus? She had no idea at all. Love does not count the length of its dreams. Suddenly, without her perceiving the least noise of steps or of tossed leaves, she heard a voice from the other side of the hedge, calling:

"Désirée!"

All the blood in her veins rushed back to her heart. She remained motionless, pale as if she were going to swoon. Through the hawthorn the same voice repeated:

"Désirée!"

She rose slowly then and turned around.

It was he. He had come as she had foreseen. He looked at her half hidden by the hedge, and, in his eyes, there was the confession of his love and the pride of feeling himself loved. A sprig of broom hung from the ribbon of his cap. He had not dressed himself up. He had run, on seeing her, he, the rich man, in his work-day clothes, like an honest lad who does not try to deceive.

Strange to say, it was this contrast between herself and him which first struck Désirée, and her agitation was increased. She, who barely earned her living, had decked herself out; she, whose parents, for want of bread, had had to have recourse to the charity of the Sisters. Her parasol and her lisle-thread gloves, two luxuries which she had never had before, gave her the effect of a falsehood. She was troubled. She was ashamed. Her pleasure of a moment before, her vanity at being well dressed, seemed to her ridiculous, guilty even. She began to despise herself. Without ceasing to look at the hedge, without saying a word, she took off her gloves and let them fall to the ground. The red parasol escaped from her hands and rolled on the grass. Then, when she had become again the simple work-girl, with bare hands, with cheeks exposed to the sun, in the dress which she had worn for a long time, with nothing pretentious, the true daughter of the chair-mender, a single phrase fell from her lips, a word of humble and sad love:

"I am very poor!" she said.

But he began to smile, with a kind, tender smile. Poor? He knew it very well. He liked her so. And as she stood motionless, all blushing in the growing joy of welcomed love, he put aside the branches better to see her and said:

"Come, Désirée!"

She obeyed as if he had the right to command her. Already she belonged to him. A few yards from there she found a gap; he stretched his hand to her; she passed through the hedge. A whole cloud of butterflies passed before her.

Once on the other side, Désirée did not withdraw the hand which she had given, and, holding each other thus, they began a walk around the mill, the pleasantest walk that either had ever taken.

However, Le Bolloche, coming to the place in the meadow which he had pointed out to his daughter, stopped before the red parasol, which, resting on its handle and two of its whalebones, only shaded a bunch of daisies and buttercups. He naturally concluded that Désirée was not far away; he looked for her in the meadow, found nothing there, looked over the hedge and saw her on the arm of the miller. He was not more excited than he had reason to be, knowing that his daughter was prudent and finding that the other had an honest look. His first impulse was to call them, but there were too many people around. He preferred to go and find them. So five minutes later Père Le Bolloche, Désirée, and the miller were all three talking together.

Ten minutes later it was the same. An hour passed without the subject, it appears, being exhausted. The shadow of the mill lengthened out on the knoll. The remaining seven mowers rested more and more. The chief of the squad did not return. A sister was obliged to recall him, saying:

"Well! well! Père Le Bolloche, to-day is not the day for going out!"

Then the group separated; the old man went back to the hospital. Désirée took the road to the town and the miller mounted his ladder. . . .

When night came and the little old men were in bed, Le Bolloche, whom the moonlight prevented from sleeping, awoke his neighbour to tell him:

"Père Lizourette, I am going to marry my daughter!"

"Désirée? With a zouave?"

"No."

"Then with a cavalryman?"

"No."

"Is he only in the line?" continued the neighbour, with an air of commiseration; "you are going to marry her into the line?"

"Not even that. He only did two months service, as the son of a widow. I know that is not much, but what can you do? He plays the fife in a band, where there are many old soldiers."

"Ah! he plays the fife!"

"Yes."

"It is a fine instrument!"

"Rather small," replied Le Bolloche. "But the children suit each other. I saw that, and then——"

"You have done well," said Lizourette sententiously; "one must not be hard upon the young."

And the two old soldiers, satisfied, having exhausted all their opinions, went to sleep. The ray of moonlight which looked on Le Bolloche moved over to Lizourette and thence on to the neighbouring beds, whose arrangement resembled a row of white stones. When Sister Dorothée, on her tour of inspection, passed Le Bolloche, she thought:

"How happy this old man looks; that gives me pleasure!"

At the same hour the young miller, leaning on his elbows out of his round window, was thinking, his head bathed in the bracing air which blew up from the river; and he was so happy to be alive that he, calm and taciturn by nature and not a poet at all, felt a desire to sing. He gazed far away, above the city, to a point of the horizon where the tiny gas-jets, farther apart than in other places, marked the beginning of the country. There his heart pictured to him the girl, radiant, laying out the straw in the sunshine, the girl whom he had chosen, the one who just now had given him her hand, the one who soon would be his wife.

And yet it was deep night and in the enclosure Désirée was not spreading out rye straw. She was standing by the bed of her grandmother, who had wished to go to bed as usual but who did not wish to go to sleep.

"Tell me again something about him," said the blind mother. "Is his hair light?"

"Rather dark," replied Désirée, laughing.

"A jolly face?"

"Rather."

"I like that," continued the old woman. "My departed was the same. Does he talk much?"

"That depends. With me, he scarcely stopped."

"Look at her, this child, how proud she is to be young! And you say that he has some property?"

"Oh, yes! a great deal, Grandmother, much more than we!"

"But do you know, I cannot get used to the

idea, my daughter! What did you do to please him?"

Désirée laughed with all her heart, with a laugh which said: "Why, Grandmother, if you could see me!" And in truth the humble mender of chairs was beautiful, all beaming with a deep and calm joy. When the grandmother had ceased to chatter, when she herself succeeded in going to sleep in the early hours of the morning, she dreamed charming dreams: that the mill had new wings; that there were four bouquets of orange blossoms at the end of the arms; that she stood in the door, beautifully dressed, and that the children, coming out of school, passed before her and bowed to her saying:

"Good day, Madame!"

VII.

The grandmother had reason to be glad, for it had been agreed, by express stipulation, at the request of Désirée, that the young household should live in the house of the meadow. Her old age would be well sheltered between these two, who would take care of her. She would assuredly have her share in their happiness, as an old-topped tree in an orchard, upon which others, full of sap, let their petals fall, so that one imagines that it still has blossoms. This miller of the white mill was an honest youth, accommodating and very much in love, since he was willing to go every morning and every evening over the road which separated his mill from the faubourg. All was rose-coloured in that quarter; there were no people so happy to be young as Désirée and her fiancé, nor any old woman less sad to be old than Grandmother Le Bolloche. But at the Little Sisters of the Poor a cloud darkened the humour of the old sergeant. After a few days of perfect content he had suddenly sunk into a profound melancholy. What was the matter? Was he sorry to give up his daughter? Why, no! The sacrifice was consummated, he was even more and more accustomed to the hospital, to his comrades, to the abundant coffee of the sisters, to their cares, to the sunny *far niente* of the field of rye. Had his future son-in-law offended him? In no way. Le Bolloche suffered from what had held and still held so great a place in his life: from the want of the plume. He was vain. In his limited mind, the mind of a former sergeant decked with braid and with chevrons, he turned over now at every hour of the day the same complaint, which he confided to no one.

"What sort of a figure will I cut at Désirée's wedding, fitted out as I am, with a chopped-off jacket, my trousers too short, my shoes, my zouave cap worn out and without a crown? Is that full dress? The relatives and friends that they will invite in numbers will laugh at me, for it will be a beautiful fête. Those who have not seen me for twenty years will be ashamed to recognise me, and even Désirée, good daughter as she is, will not be flattered in her new wedding-dress, to have such a sorry-looking father by her side. Better not to go. No, I will not go!"

And already he had begun to prepare his comrades in arms and in the last asylum for this desperate resolution.

"I shall probably not go," he said to them. "I have a deuce of a rheumatism in my shoulder!" But they did not believe a word of it. Rheumatism, he! Go along! When he was walking by himself, they saw him from the distance twirl his cane about, cutting off with a sharp blow the heads of thistles growing on the edge of the field. The very vigour of the twirl was enough to prove that Le Bolloche lied; it also showed a violent state of mind, which the sisters, naturally, were not without remarking.

"I do not know what ails our little Père Le Bolloche?" remarked Sister Dorothée; "he eats well, he drinks well, he sleeps well, he had his supply of tobacco again day before yesterday; and yet he does not seem happy!"

As a matter of fact, the poor pensioners who are thus cared for usually find nothing to complain of. As she was a woman and a very inquisitive one, —which no vow prevents—she wished to know. One morning as she was dressing one of his companions—for Le Bolloche dressed himself without help—she plied the latter with adroitly put questions. She did not ask him outright: "What is the matter?" No, but already suspecting that the wedding of Désirée was the cause of his trouble, she said:

"I hope, Le Bolloche, that you will be happy to see your daughter a bride."

"Without doubt," growled Le Bolloche.

"And where will the wedding take place? In the meadow, I wager."

"Yes."

"They will dance?"

"Yes."

"And you will open the dance, of course?"

Le Bolloche could contain himself no longer.

"Dressed—like this, yes, will I?" he cried. "A former non-commissioned officer of zouaves! I look as if I should dance there—I shall not even go!"

"Oh," said the sister, smiling, "how vain you are!"

She who had never been vain! Le Bolloche did not take the jest in good part. The wrinkle at both corners of his mouth deepened.

"I am nothing but a beggar here," he cried; "my time is past, past. I have no wish to appear in the world any more, and that is it!"

He walked away with long strides, fuming with rage. Sister Dorothée followed him with her eyes, a smile lengthened her lips, a smile in which there was pity and pleasure at having been adroit, and also the radiance of a sweet thought which she had just had. She made haste to dress Père Lizourette; she tied his cravat, which she amused herself in arranging like the wings of a butterfly, and, handing him his cane, said: "You are handsome as a star, go amuse yourself." Then she left the ward, directing her steps toward the superior's room. Along the broad silent corridors she glided lightly as if borne on the wings of the thought which had come to her.

Three weeks passed in this way, during which Le Bolloche became more and more sad.

At last the day fixed for the wedding of Désirée arrived.

On that morning Le Bolloche, who had scarcely slept, rose a little before the others and went out under the pretext of going to dig in his garden. But scarcely outside, he stopped; he sought in the distance the country where his poor mind had wandered all night. From the hill of the hospital, old as he was, he could not distinguish the house. But in the blue mist of the morning he made out the white spot which the faubourg made, and the pale-green masses which were the orchards. A pure breath of air came from them. The poor old man felt his eyes fill with tears, and he imagined that he heard, carried by the wind, a voice which said:

"Come, Father, get up; come, it is my wedding-day. Grandmother has a new dress, which my fiancé gave her. For me, I am beautiful as the day. I have a wreath of wax flowers, a figured shawl and a brooch to fasten it; above all, my heart is full of joy, for in three hours we will start to be married. Come, I wish to kiss you very hard for having given me life, which is so sweet now, life which opens like a fête. Come and see my happiness!"

Le Bolloche, agitated, his mind half wandering, hesitated a moment; then he recovered his senses, shook his head, gave the faubourg a last look and repeated what he had not ceased to say:

"No, I will not go!"

He began walking down to the rear of the enclosure, where his garden was, but he had not taken thirty steps when some one tapped him on the shoulder. He turned around. It was his wife.

"Husband," she said, "come with me!"

"Where to?"

"Come to the parlour before going home!"

"We have no home."

"Come just the same; you will see."

Usually he did not comply readily with the requests of his wife, but he was so dejected and she seemed to be in such good spirits that, partly from indifference, partly from the attraction of a partial surprise, he followed her. When they reached the door of the parlour near the entrance, Mère Le Bolloche stood by the wall and let her husband pass.

"Enter, Le Bolloche," she said, "and let us dress for the wedding."

The good man entered and stopped stupefied. He had just discovered, carefully folded on the back of a chair, a complete suit, handsomer than any he had worn since he had been in civil life: a grey pair of trousers, still fresh; a waistcoat, a black frock coat, a light cravat with blue polka dots, and a silk hat which had endured more than one ironing, but was still upright on its base and very similar in form to that of the former shako, which could not fail to please an old soldier like Le Bolloche. The latter, without more hesitation, began to dress. Everything fitted well; one would have sworn that a tailor had taken his measure. When he put his hand in his trousers pocket, he drew out a piece of silver. When he crossed the wide lapels of his frock coat upon his breast, his military medal shone there, attached by a new ribbon.

During this time the little old woman put on a cotton dress with wide plaits; pinned a yellow handkerchief with brown stripes, brilliant and shaded like an African pink, upon her breast; fastened the ties of a ruched cap, ornamented with two blue bows. Decidedly, Sister Dorothée had forgotten nothing. So many fine things represented for her many hours of work, many late nights, since the sisters have no leisure in the daytime for these exceptional, fond indulgences.

Le Bolloche felt his heart swell with emotion in thinking of it. He recalled the harsh words which he had many times spoken. Tears came to his eyes, and he had all the trouble in the world to keep them back; for an old sergeant never weeps.

But when they came out of the parlour and he saw in the courtyard his cart freshly painted, the donkey harnessed, combed, dressed for Sunday too, with red pompons on the blinders, the poor old man could not control his feelings; great tears rolled down his cheeks. He went straight up to Sister Dorothée, who was standing at the head of the equipage, and took her hand.

"Sister!" he exclaimed with a stifled voice.

"What is it, my good man?"

"Sister, this is religion and the true kind. I know it, you can believe me, for I have travelled much! Yes, the true——"

He could not finish. But the sister understood perfectly. He got into the cart, made his wife sit down beside him, and touched up the donkey.

After a few paces he stopped the animal, turned around and, with a face this time beaming, called again:

"Sister Dorothée, since it appears that it will give you pleasure, I will dance at the wedding of Désirée."

"Be good!" replied the sister.

And as she watched the couple ride off to the slow trot of the donkey between the walls of the neighbouring street, the sister felt a longing to weep in her turn, feeling indeed that she had won the heart of the old zouave, the most difficult of her "little old men."

THE RAPHAEL OF MONSIEUR PRUNELIER.

THE RAPHAEL OF MONSIEUR PRUNELIER.

I.

Why was he walking along the bank of the Aulne, he who never walked for pleasure? Why sauntering leisurely along the pleasant path, bordered with beech-trees, which leads from Port-Launay to Châteaulin, with beaming countenance, nodding with a paternal gesture to the washerwomen who were kneeling at intervals on the sloping bank and who stopped beating the linen long enough to say: "*Bon jour*, Monsieur Piédouche!"

That is a point which no one can explain. Monsieur Piédouche, for thirty years banker at Châteaulin, wealthy, influential, and esteemed, never confided his affairs to any one. A despatch from the Stock Exchange that afternoon had put him in a good humour; that is all that the best-informed of his clerks knew. He left his office and after an hour's walk was now returning, pleased with himself, the weather, the landscape—filled with overflowing sympathy for the beggars of the street. His joy found expression in every way, in alms, bows, smiles, in humming or whistling refrains of his youth. Bubbling over with happiness, he was seized with an irresistible desire to buy something, and an engraving in the rue du Tribunal catching his eye, he stopped.

The engraving, exposed with several others in the low window of an old house, was plainly a Nicholas Berghem. The subject was a group of trees half stripped of their leaves, a ford, a woman on a donkey, a fleecy sky—the whole in the most pleasing style and precisely in the key in which the spirit of Monsieur Piédouche was pitched.

"I am going to give pleasure to two persons," he thought: "to myself, in the first place, and then to poor Monsieur Prunelier."

He ascended the three moss-grown steps, worn on the edges where so many generations had trod, and rung the bell. The mistress of the house answered the bell. She was plainly not a woman of the country. Her fair hair rolled back over a shell comb, something alert and quick in her movements, a youthful look, in spite of the forty years which had marked the rosy face with fine crossed lines, her speech, too, so quick and without accent—in short, her whole personality was different from that of the provincial woman. As soon as she had ushered Monsieur Piédouche into the drawing-room, she seated herself upon a low chair, her back against the light.

"You wish to see Monsieur Prunelier?" she asked.

"No, Madame."

"What a pity!" she continued, without heeding the reply; "my husband is out, I do not expect him home before six o'clock this evening. But he will go to your house, you know. His terms are the very lowest: for a simple crayon five francs only for a sitting, and likeness guaranteed; naturally oil is dearer. I strongly advise you to have oil. Oil is Monsieur Prunelier's specialty. Félix has so much talent!"

"You are mistaken," interrupted the banker. "I have no intention of having my portrait painted. I came in merely to ask the price of the engraving in the window below."

The poor woman had hoped something more from the visit of the banker. Sensitive, like those who have known better days, she held up her head and replied with a somewhat piqued air:

"The Berghem of Monsieur Prunelier is not for sale."

The banker, who was a kind-hearted man, rose and, desiring to take his leave graciously, pointed to three paintings hanging above the sofa of worn cretonne: "Samples of your famous collection, Madame Prunelier? They are beautiful paintings!"

"They are by Lancret," she replied with indifference; "the French school. Lancret is a master much sought after at sales."

"Very much sought after," repeated the banker vaguely, not knowing much about it, but still desirous of leaving an agreeable impression.

"Would you care to visit the gallery?" asked Madame Prunelier at once.

He accepted. He was not sorry to see this collection which had a reputation throughout Finistère and which caused the people of Châteaulin to say: "You know, whenever the Pruneliers want to have an income, it will be easy for them."

Madame Prunelier led the way; she left him for an instant standing before a door, while she went for the key, came back, opened the door and stood aside that the banker might enter first and receive better "the shock of the masters."

It was dazzling, in fact, at first sight. From the four walls of the room hung with paintings in gilded frames, sparks flashed forth, a diffusion of red and yellow gold, and mingled with tiny glints from the varnish, with reflections from brilliant draperies, trailing from the inclined canvases and stretching out on the white and brown parquetry, a fine inlaid floor on which the three windows of the façade were reflected as in a mirror.

A second surprise followed. Each picture bore the name of the artist upon a scroll. And what names! The greatest of all schools, of all ages, grouped together by a magic wand which had not forgotten any! Ruysdael elbowed Hobbema; a beggar of Ribera invoked a Virgin of Leonardo; two paintings of Perugini flanked a triptych of the elder Holbein. There were smaller canvases by Teniers, Potter, Fragonard. Certain ones, a very few, joined with an "Anonymous" which greatly lessened their importance, were placed in the corners, bearing the legend: "Venetian School," "Florentine School," "Flemish School."

"All these have been discovered, restored, and retouched by Monsieur Prunelier," said the lady after a moment; "Félix has so much talent!"

Then perceiving how little artistic discernment was shown by Monsieur Piédouche, who only paused before the carved frames, she exclaimed amiably:

"This one is our Poussin, French school, 'The Kiss of Saint Dominic and Saint Francis.'"

The banker thought to himself that the two saints looked like two rogues, but was not rude enough to say so.

"This one here," continued the hostess, "is a painting of the first order: 'The Combat,' by Salvator Rosa. Notice what relief, what life! Rothschild would have had this long ago had we been willing."

This seemed greatly to impress Monsieur Piédouche. He examined the painting very closely. The rumps of three horses occupied the foreground, and behind these dappled-grey rotundities a frightful conflict of factions appeared to be taking place.

"Then you were not willing?" he asked.

"Naturally."

He lifted his eyebrows in a way which showed that he did not comprehend in the least why Monsieur Prunelier had not yielded to the entreaties of Rothschild.

"Where is it signed?" he asked. "I have so little knowledge of paintings that I do not know even whether one should look for the signature on the right or the left."

The poor man was ignorant that these searches for paternity in private collections are usually in the worst taste. Madame Prunelier made him conscious of this.

"You should know," she said, "that Salvator rarely ever signed. After all, what does a signature amount to? It is the brush, Monsieur, the composition, the colouring, which are the true signature, that which cannot be imitated!"

Under this shower of censures, Monsieur Piédouche continued his way along the same wall. Only he made more haste.

Madame Prunelier was silent, and let him walk along. But when she saw that her visitor was approaching the last panel, that he was on the point of passing perhaps without noticing it, this masterpiece, enshrined in an open-worked, carved ebony frame, she could not resist the temptation of rejoining him and resuming her rôle of cicerone.

"A Raphael!" she murmured in a slow, dreamy voice, suffused with emotion. She waited.

However determined Monsieur Piédouche was not to show the slightest sign of scepticism again, he gave a slight start at this name.

"You are amazed! Every one feels the same!" continued Madame Prunelier in the same stifled tone. "Yes, Monsieur, a Raphael Sanzio! a copy of this Madonna is in the Naples Museum."

The banker bowed.

"I say a copy truly. Some amateurs of Châteaulin recently visited Naples and saw the copy; on their return, they declared to me, standing here in the very place where you are: 'It is beautiful, Madame Prunelier, but it is not like this! In your gallery one feels that they are in the presence of the original.' That is exactly what you have just experienced. I watched for that movement of the shoulders, that shiver of authenticity, as my husband terms it."

The worthy man, grown prudent, did not breathe a word. She looked at him for an instant and concluded with this phrase, which was a warning:

"Besides, the Raphael of Monsieur Prunelier has never been questioned!"

Monsieur Piédouche had no desire to question the Raphael. He passed down the stairs and was on the point of taking leave of Madame Prunelier when the door opened and Monsieur Prunelier, tall and ungainly, his hat on his head, came in like a whirlwind. Monsieur Prunelier's eyes were set wide apart, giving him a grim look. He fastened one of them on the banker and his glance asked: "What kind of a man is he? Oil? Crayon? Simple cockney!"

"Monsieur has just visited our gallery," replied his wife.

Monsieur Prunelier shrugged his shoulders, vexed no doubt at having wasted so much time on a bourgeois, pushed open the door of the drawing-room with his hand and disappeared, saying:

"I wish to speak to you, Valentine."

Then as soon as he was alone with her in the dining-room adjoining the drawing-room, where she had followed in haste and anxious, he cried, still tragic:

"Valentine, there is going to be an Exposition of Fine Arts at Châteaulin!"

She divined the unexpressed thought of the master. Something sorrowful and tender passed over her face and, wishing to be certain, she said: "Well, Félix?"

He was still theatrical when he answered:

"I have decided! I will exhibit it! I wish to sell it. Do not forbid me!"

But she was natural and touching when she thanked him, saying, her eyes moist with great tears:

"You are generous, Félix, you are brave. It is well!"

But emotion was not lasting with either of them. They sat down to table before a slice of pâté and a plate of cherries, found that they were hungry, and began talking and laughing about Monsieur Piédouche, about the provincial bourgeois, as they had not talked or laughed for twenty years, not since the golden age when, on Sunday, in a corner of Clamart or Meudon, fatigued by a long walk through the woods, with pockets full of nuts and hearts full of hope, they dined under sunny trellises, facing hazy Paris.

II.

It is a long way from Paris to Châteaulin! How had they, he Gascon, she Parisienne, both Bohemians and crazy about the great city, ever come to run aground there? What reason had led them to choose this corner of Brittany—the most common one, alas? After ten years spent in expectation of a medal from the Salon, the medal failed to come; the dot of Madame Prunelier was consumed; Monsieur Prunelier was soured. During the winter they lived a life of makeshifts; in summer, for the sake of economy, they travelled in the poor districts, where they found hotels at four francs, candles included. Prunelier continued his work of painting landscapes which never sold. It happened that once, at Châteaulin to be precise, some one ordered a portrait from him. The order was scarcely finished when there came a second, then a third. People begged him to restore the portraits of their ancestors. Women of the world addressed him as: "My dear Monsieur Prunelier," and many suggested that he should open a school of design. He was flattered. He fancied that the vein would never be exhausted, and he settled down in the midst of his models.

And now he had lived at Châteaulin for ten years, less and less occupied. His wife took care of him, nursed him in the tepid atmosphere of illusions which suited his childish nature. She was a worthy woman, endowed with the energy of the Parisian women, who are models of patience, of invention, of courage in the struggle with poverty. You can readily guess that she had often thought of selling the Raphael. It would have been so good to have no more debts, to live liberally, to be able to buy curtains for the windows, and the fur cape which she coveted; to have flowers in profusion, and—who knows—to dare to say to Monsieur Prunelier on waking some morning: "Félix, your youth and mine are calling us yonder. Do you hear them singing on both banks of the Seine—our twenty years of love, our long hopes, our many friendships and many delightful hours, the poorest of which I regret now? Come, let us be off, will you, since we are rich?" Yes, she had dreamed of all that very often, without ever putting it in words. The sacrifice of alienating the gem of his collection would have been too cruel for Monsieur Prunelier, and the worthy woman displayed not a little of her tenderness in never hinting at such a separation.

But now! Now that he had resolved of his own accord to exhibit his masterpiece, to sell it, witness this human weakness: she had no longer the courage to say no; she felt a joy for which she reproached herself; the Raphael became odious to her; she would be glad to know that it was far away, in the château of one of those English lords who pay fabulous prices for rare works of art. Would this exposition never begin?

The day came, however, as all days, desired or not, do come. In the great hall of the civil court, then in recess, artists of every class, especially those who frequent the Breton coast, had sent countless apple-trees in bloom, numbers of marine views with a flame of light trailing over the waters, fisherwomen of Feyen-Perrin, peasant girls bearing a likeness to those of Jules Breton, and five or six canvases, huge since they treated of history, and a still life. Upon a panel reserved in the midst of old paintings loaned from the châteaux of Finistère, and filling its space, were the three pearls of Monsieur Prunelier: the Poussin, the Salvator Rosa, and the Raphael. These three names, freshly gilded, glistened at the foot of the frames. A pennant of cardboard under them, extending out three yards in length, bore the inscription: "From the gallery of M. Prunelier (Félix), artist, at Châteaulin. For sale."

The artist, his exhibitor's card fastened by a rubber and dangling from his buttonhole, came and went as in his own house, at any hour, without paying, which fact rejoiced him every time. People stared at him a great deal. He remained there whole afternoons, mingling with groups of visitors, trying to seize a word of praise, if need be to call it forth, and ready to reply to the offers of purchasers, for crowds of people visited the exposition. Bills placarded in all the towns of the west summoned the people to visit the "Fêtes of Châteaulin on the occasion of the Fine Arts Exposition." The newspapers, even those of Paris, applauded this trial of "artistic decentralisation" and Monsieur Prunelier, exultant, had read to his wife these lines taken from one of them: "The gem of the Exposition is without dispute the Raphael from the collection of Monsieur Prunelier, one of the most distinguished amateurs of Châteaulin. This superb canvas is for sale. We would like to hope that the Administration of the Fine Arts will not a second time let itself be forestalled by foreign competition, and that our Louvre, so poor . . ." etc.

From that moment, Madame Prunelier never left the house.

"You understand, Valentine," the painter had said, "a delegate from the Fine Arts Administration may come here. He must find some one to talk with. I shall be at the Exposition. Do not budge from the house, so that we shall not miss him."

She had faithfully observed the order; she trembled at every peal of the bell, imagined a hundred times that she saw him pass the house, as her husband fancied that he recognised him among the visitors.

"That must have been he," she said; "that tall, slender man with decorations, and with a portfolio. He seemed to be a stranger in Châteaulin."

"He did not come in?"

"No."

"Doubtless he went to the hotel. He will come to-morrow, Valentine."

The month passed; the Exposition closed; the delegate had not appeared. Monsieur Prunelier began to speak in the harshest terms of "that Administration, the most indifferent in Europe," when, one morning, as he was working alone in the little dining-room, the postman brought a letter of elongated form bearing a foreign stamp. At once Monsieur Prunelier comprehended that the decisive hour had come. There was the printed address of the sender upon the envelope: "Thos. Shepherd and Sons, dealers in antique paintings, 253 Southampton Street, London." Beneath this, in an admirable English handwriting: "Monsieur Prunelier (Félix)," and in a corner the word "Confidential." The painter tore it open, uttered a cry, and began dancing about the room.

Ten minutes seemed an hour to him. When he

heard the grating of the key in the lock, he threw himself in front of his wife, who had returned from market.

"Sold!" he cried, "sold!"

She turned very pale, and staggering, without saying a word, followed her husband into the dining-room. He closed the doors, made her sit down near the table, took both her hands in his, and while his eyes, his mobile nostrils, his mouth, hidden in the waves of his grey beard, and his whole face beamed, he repeated:

"Do you understand? Sold!"

She smiled with an effort like a person who is not mistress of her first emotion and who still doubts:

"Really, Félix! He came then while I was out?"

"No, a letter came from a large firm in London. So much the worse for the Administration! You do not think that I should wait any longer?"

"Oh, no!" she cried eagerly, "I beseech you!"

"It is a sacrifice for me, Valentine. My patriotism suffers at the thought of it; to see a masterpiece like that pass into the hands of foreigners, a masterpiece!"

"How much do they offer you?" she interrupted. And in the glance she fixed upon her husband one could have read that it was the question of poverty or of a happy life which she was asking. He turned away his eyes and said, letting his fingers slip over the table:

"*Mon Dieu!* it is not a fortune—much less than it is worth—eight hundred francs."

Madame Prunelier bounded from her chair:

"Eight hundred francs! The Raphael!"

"No, my dear," replied Monsieur Prunelier, lowering his voice, "the Raphael—with the Poussin and the Salvator. I confess it—it is very——"

"What are you saying? For the three! Why, it is a joke, a frightful cheat—or indeed then your collection is——"

"Valentine!"

"Well, what is one to think? That passes the limit indeed! Eight hundred francs for a Raphael that has never been questioned! How many times have you told me that it had never been——"

"They do not question it, my dear! They write explicitly: 'Your Raphael, your Poussin, your Salvator!' Look at it. The trouble is that there is no demand for art any longer; no more at London than at Châteaulin! Is it my fault? Oh! why did you come in? I was so happy a few moments ago!"

Great tears rolled down the cheeks of the painter, dropping upon his shaggy beard. He looked so unhappy that his wife pitied him. She went up to him and kissed him.

"My poor Félix," she cried, "I had foolish ideas, you see. That Madonna represented a fortune to me. After all, eight hundred francs is something certainly! It will help us very much."

Already he was consoled, this old baby whom a caress appeased and a word of hope carried off into dreamland.

"You are an admirable woman!" he exclaimed, "a true wife for an artist! You may be sure that

I am going to work hard, yes, indeed! You will see. It gives me courage to see a little water come to the mill. For you have just said with truth eight hundred francs is something! I shall buy you a cloak for the winter, the first thing."

"No, no, Félix, I do not want one."

"But since I offer it to you, Valentine! We will discuss that later. Let us go for a walk now, will you?"

Monsieur Prunelier took his wife's arm and drew her outside. He needed to show his joy. And the day without was truly of exquisite and tempting clearness; the gillyflowers along the worn walls of the old courts were drinking in the sunshine. The streams of light, which searched every place, silvered the fragments of mica in the granite of the sombre houses. The large windows, with their tiny panes, were open on each side of the street; and the housewives, whom the mere sound of footsteps attracts, looked down astonished to see Monsieur Prunelier, who was walking slowly, contrary to his custom, his head uplifted, rejuvenated, with the air of a new man among new things.

They were not mistaken. He was walking in the full vision of the future. It is true he was no longer twenty, but life still stretched out a long way before him; above all, he was happy. With the price of his Raphael, he was buying a bond and likewise a suit of blue fine-twilled flannel, ample and soft, a morning suit fit for a gentleman artist.

He even saw a pupil in his enlarged studio; a

pupil with a pointed beard, come to study under his direction, to learn how to transfer and to restore works of art. For in these days he thought much less of making himself the head of a school and of preparing for the Prix de Rome. Madame Prunelier listened to him, still sad from the disappointment that she had experienced, but also pleased to see his happiness. They met Monsieur Piédouche, and Monsieur Prunelier accosted him familiarly:

"You remember that Raphael that you did not take seriously?" he said.

"Well?"

"It is sold to England."

"Is it possible?"

"As I tell you. All the profits, you see, are not in banks, Monsieur Piédouche: art has its returns, too!"

The banker was a kind man. He replied with sincerity:

"So much the better, Monsieur Prunelier, so much the better!"

The couple continued their walk. They crossed the Aulne, turned to the left, and went up by the path which the pardon processions follow, to the hills overlooking the little town. They sat down. The river made a bend at their feet; a double wall of trees turned with it; here and there wooded heights loomed up in the vast horizon; the sky was blue.

"It looks a little like Saint-Germain," said Monsieur Prunelier. "Do you recollect the day after our marriage when we walked upon the terrace? I was twenty-four. How pretty you were, Valentine! It was a bright day like this; do you remember it?"

For the moment Madame Prunelier was caught in the snare of recollections. Both travelled far back into the joyous past; both agreed that life has its sweet hours, and when they went down the hill, a long time after, Châteaulin received a little smile like that of former days from Madame Prunelier, a smile that was intended for Saint-Germain-en-Laye.

From that time Monsieur Prunelier began to expect the payment for his Raphael with the confiding tranquillity of those who have usually only creditors.

III.

Three months later the painter, sick with poverty and with grief, was forced to keep his bed. Alas! That great English firm! It had had the audacity, some weeks after the delivery of the paintings, to claim the frames, all three antique, which Monsieur Prunelier had believed himself authorised to keep, in view of the low price for the paintings. The firm gave him to understand that, as soon as this condition was fulfilled, payment would follow. The poor man had sent the frames on to rejoin Salvator, Raphael, and Poussin. But nothing had come back in return; not one penny! Wasted and dejected, he was lying in his curtainless iron bed a prey to fever. The famous cloak of imitation fur, bought on credit, which covered his feet in the guise of an eiderdown, the paper of the room, loose and hanging from the wall in places, the chair rounds and bits of board smouldering in the chimney-place, everything around him proclaimed a poverty against which one struggles no more.

It was the end! What was the use of mending; what was the good of keeping things? The master was dying! In order to buy medicine for him, or some sweets which he liked, Madame Prunelier deprived herself of food.

She forced herself to give him courage and, although she had not had the slightest ray of hope for a long time, she often talked as if she had. Her turn had come to call the future to the aid of the present; twenty times a day she would go up to the invalid and say with a faint smile:

"I do not know why, Félix, but I have an idea that we shall be paid? Some one was saying yesterday that nothing was lost! What a pleasure it will be, will it not, as soon as you are better, to go and cash the bill of exchange? We will pay our debts, Félix, all our debts, and there is sure to be something left; I have calculated that there would be something left."

But he had lost faith in life. She looked at him, turned away; already the smile had vanished.

One evening the bell rang, and Monsieur Piédouche was ushered up. His face wore a discreetly beaming smile as he entered the sick-chamber; his watch-charms moved upon his panting breast. On seeing him seat himself at the foot of the bed, the sick man raised himself upon his elbow. A lightning-flash of his proud youth as a fierce artist, a gleam of his old dislike for the bourgeois, blazed in his eyes.

"How are you, Monsieur Prunelier?" asked the banker.

"Poorly, Monsieur."

"What is the trouble?"

"My mainspring is broken."

"*Sapristi!* This is not the moment for that! Our affairs are going well."

"Not mine—always——"

"But here is the proof, my dear sir."

The banker took four bank-notes from his pocketbook and tendered them to the poor Bohemian. Monsieur Prunelier, who had instinctively reached out his hand, withdrew it with dignity.

"By what right, if you please?" he demanded.

The other coloured slightly and said:

"Why—it is an instalment from the English firm."

"Shepherd & Sons?"

"Precisely."

"That is all right, Monsieur; pardon me, I thought that it might be charity."

The poor man seized the bank-bills, counted them, turned them over, arranged them one after the other on his bed. You would have said that he had taken a new lease of life. The despondency from which nothing had roused him until then disappeared by degrees; he began to talk and chatted for more than a quarter of an hour. A glimmer of gaiety even touched him, and he recovered his bantering studio tone enough to say to the banker when he was taking his leave:

"Joker! You see now that I was not mistaken! It was a large firm!"

Illusions, smiling queens of the world, how this man belonged to you!

He died. But he left by will to his widow, "In return for her unalterable devotion in good as in evil fortune," all his property, personal and real estate, in full ownership, notably the balance of the credit of Shepherd & Sons, of London.

The banker paid a second time, with the same money doubtless as the first, without requiring a commission.

Madame Prunelier, grateful for his kind treatment, begged Monsieur Piédouche to accept the Berghem engraving.

It was in his house that I saw it, hanging in the banker's library above the scales with which he weighs gold—a pretty Dutch landscape, with its mill, its river, its pale sun, discreet as a smile of pity.

Monsieur Piédouche prizes it highly. He looks at it with a pleasure in which its art has little share, for one day when some one asked him:

"How much did you give for it?"

He answered thoughtlessly:

"Eight hundred francs."

And at the other's exclamation of surprise, the worthy man added:

"I would not sell it for double the money."